Th

Adventures of Steve
Revenge of Herobrine

Abir Gupta

Nitya Publications

First Edition 2023

ISBN: 978-81-19147-93-9

Published & Printed by:
Nitya Publications, Bhopal MP India
Web: www.nityapublications.com
Email: info@nityapublications.com
Mob: 9009291840

Disclaimer

This book has been published with all reasonable efforts to make the material error-free after the author's consent. No part of this book shall be used or reproduced in any manner. The author of this book is solely responsible and liable for its content, including but not limited to the views, representations, descriptions, statements, information, opinions, and references ["Content"].

This book is a work of fan-fiction; it is not an official Minecraft book. It is not endorsed, authorized, licensed, sponsored, or supported by Mojang AB, Microsoft Corporation or any other entity owning or controlling right to the Minecraft name, trademarks or copyrights.

The Content of this book shall not constitute or be construed or deemed to reflect the opinion or expression of the Publisher or Editor.

This book is sold subject to the condition that it shall not, by way of trade or otherwise, be lent, resold, reprint, re-distribute, hired out, or otherwise circulated, without the publisher's prior consent, in any form of binding or cover other than that it is originally published.

Contents

Have Fun Reading.

The Revenge of Herobrine

<u>Chapter 1</u>

He was falling in the bottomless abyss for what seemed like hours. How long had he been in the void for? Further below him, an inanimate human was evidently taking damage until he disappeared into the menacing darkness. It was only a matter of time before he was swallowed into the chaos. Herobrine had one more option. Gathering all his might, he teleported back to the Overworld.

It was night. The silver stars shimmered in the sky softly and the only sound in the clear night air was Herobrine's footsteps. He felt weak. After all his planning, this had happened. Steve and Alex had defeated the Ender dragon and he'd been thrown into the void. Herobrine knew he was vulnerable at the moment; he needed shelter and fast. He also needed the one thing he thought he would never require- the help of some very bad eggs.

Not having the energy to teleport, Herobrine sagged down beside a tree and fell into a deep slumber...

Meanwhile, Steve and Alex were bathing in triumph after Herobrine had been defeated. Jay might not have been with them, but he was always in their memories. Steve and Alex were both stocked up with experience points after taking down the dragon and had the dragon egg as a memento. But as far as they could tell, it didn't do anything apart from sit there like a piece of old furniture collecting dust. Maybe one day it would hatch?

"Finally! Peace at last." declared Steve. "I've had quite enough adventure for one lifetime, don't you think?"

Alex smiled. "Yeah. But now everyone can return to their normal lives. And, with Herobrine defeated we've got nothing to worry about. He's gone forever."

Or was he?

******

Chapter 2

PRESENT DAY

It was a beautiful summer's day in the village of Daint. However, Steve and Alex had other plans than picnicking. Kitted out in diamond armour, they were going back to the End for some resources. Plus, Lofty, their Enderman friend, was going to tour them around the End cities. What better to go to another dimension full of floating islands and vicious dragons for a summer vacation?

"Right. We're ready!" Steve called out to Alex who was still rummaging through chests inside. "Glass bottles; check, pickaxe; check, ender pearls; check."

"Ok. Let's go!" called Alex. Waving goodbye to the village Elder, the two friends set of for the End portal. It was quite a while away but with the aid of their ender pearls they got to the stronghold before nightfall. The last time they had been here, Alex and Steve had lit the way to the portal room up with torches. And, sure enough, they had soon reached the End portal.

"Here goes!" shouted Steve as he leapt into the rippling mass of stars. Alex followed behind him. The place was just like they remembered. The obsidian pillars bore no end crystals and many arrows were stuck near the top of them. The land around the Ender dragon's perch was blown into craters by the beds. But, most importantly, the Ender dragon's magic was still evident in places. This is what Steve and Alex needed.

Carefully approaching the damage areas, Steve bottled up all the magic and ended up with dragon's breath. Just what they needed for the most advanced potions!

After bottling the ingredient, Steve and Alex headed out to the portal leading to the outer End islands. They had planned to meet up with him there. Pillaring up closer to the portal, Alex and Steve warped into the portal where they would reunite with one of their dearest friends.

******

Chapter 3

Lofty threw his arms around Steve and Alex in a welcome-hug. "Nice to see you to, buddy." chuckled Steve. "Now what did you want to show us?" The three of them were standing on a small chunk of Endstone between two larger islands. Lofty led them over to the end of the floating island.

Ahead, there were hundreds of peculiar purple trees called chorus trees. This was the primary vegetation in the End. The crooked chorus trees grew chorus fruit which had the ability to teleport any person or mob once eaten. Alex went up to one of the trees, breaking off a piece of fruit. Before Lofty could stop her, Alex had already been teleported a few blocks away, landing hardly on the Endstone.

Steve let out a laugh as Lofty led the two towards possibly the most intriguing structure in the world: the end cities. These complex buildings were many stories high, branching off at points like chorus trees. These skyscrapers skeletal frame consisted of Endstone bricks and purpur pillars. It was a sight to behold.

Steve, Alex and Lofty approached the mystical structure. Who knew what kind of loot was inside?

But, before they entered, Lofty said,' Watch the Shulkers. They aren't exactly friendly!' On cue, a small piece of Endstone came flying at Steve. Immediately, he started levitating, flying higher every second. 'Don't panic!" Lofty said to Steve. Steve was getting increasingly flustered as he floated towards the highest spire. Lofty quickly snapped off a piece of chorus fruit and threw it at him. Steve ate it, teleporting back to the ground.

Breathing a sigh of relief, Steve inspected the thing inside the Shulker shell. It was a small, slug- like *thing*. The Shulker violently shut its shell. Parallel to it was another Shulker just like it, acting as guards. Lofty wedged open the Shulker shell and flicked the creature inside it away.

'Now we can continue.' he said, leading the way inside the city. The first floor consisted of a obstacle staircase leading upwards. Warping up, Steve and Alex scaled a ladder up towards the loot chests. Lofty beckoned them to open it. Inside, there were enchanted diamond leggings for both of them, plus some gold and diamonds.

"Cool!" commented Steve, tucking away the loot. This went on for a few hours as the trio went around raiding other end cities (hopefully the Shulkers didn't mind). Before leaving, Lofty teleported Alex and Steve up onto the last structure on the island; the end ship. It was a small ship hovering above the void. Like the End cities, it was made of Purpur pillars and Endstone bricks. It had a tall mast and a Shulker guarding the deck.

Lofty showed them the all the treasure onboard. Below the deck was a brewing stand with two potions of healing. After dealing with another Shulker, Steve and Alex feasted their eyes on the loot. The item frame above yet another two loot chest held elytra. This useful item allowed the wearer to glide across the void and other forms of tricky landscapes. "Hey, I've had one of these before!" exclaimed Steve, thinking back to the time when he first met Lofty on his quest to find the Legendary Lake. 'Take it,' Lofty said to Alex. She grabbed the elytra off the frame and swapped it for her chestplate. Leaping out from the deck, Alex soared above the archipelago, whooping with delight.

"This is so awesome!" Alex shouted as she landed smoothly on top of the crow's nest. The countless islands stretching into the distance were visible as Alex brushed the stars at the tip of the world. After taking turns with the elytra, Steve and Alex wrapped up and, along with Lofty, teleported to the Overworld via the End portal. It was deadly silent when they got back. There wasn't a sound. The usual chirpy birch forests close to Daint were always flooded with sunshine and wild animals but this wasn't right.

Steve could sense something was wrong and so could Lofty. Both of them were suspiciously looking over their shoulders every few seconds like they were being watched. Alex, on the other hand was oblivious to either Steve or Lofty's worries, apparently not noticing the dense fog that was slowly setting over the woodland. "We should hurry," said

Steve anxiously. Lofty nodded his head as he quickened his pace.

"Oh, you two worry too much!" said Alex, smiling. "It's not like-" She broke of as a shiver ran through the forest. It was like an icy blast of wind rippling through them. Alex froze. Everyone stared into the fog, looking for danger. Nothing happened. "Uhh, Lofty, do you mind teleporting us home?" Alex asked, a little scared.

Lofty nodded and shut his eyes. Just as they were about to leave, Steve thought he saw a dark shadow behind them, a something with white eyes. Could it be?

******

Chapter 4

Steve dumped down all the stuff on the table. There was a good variety of loot. Diamonds, potions, a dragon head and elytra. Plus, they still had the dragon egg. Shadow, who was watching her owner inspect the items, suddenly jumped onto the dragon head, biting into it.

"No, Shadow stop! It's not real. There's no dragon!" Steve's pet ocelot sat back and mewed. Steve looked at the dragon head a second before putting it above his bed. Shadow eyed it suspiciously. Within half an hour, Steve had done setting everything up and had brewed himself a handful of lingering potions. Not seeing the point in staying awake much longer, Steve went to sleep.

The next morning, Steve awoke to many people bustling around, chatting urgently amongst each other. It was much too early for the whole village to be awake. Walking outside, Steve was greeted by a sea of people all trying to speak to him at once.
"What happened?" he asked. The village Elder stepped in front of everyone looking terrified. Not saying anything, he handed Steve a newspaper. It said:
MINECRAFT IS BEING TAKEN OVER BY HEROBRINE

Many of Minecraft's big cities have been under attack from Herobrine. Herobrine, along with three other conspirators spare no building, human or animal. Is this the end of Minecraft?

Below it was a picture of Herobrine along with three other villains. The caption read: Herobrine along with, Entity 303, Null and Deathlord. He had never seen Entity 303 who had a scythe while Deathlord had a wicked-looking sword. Deathlord was wearing a skeleton suit while Entity 303 had red eyes and was kitted out in white. He thought he recognized Null from somewhere, though he couldn't remember where. But one thing was clear- neither of them were human.

Steve suddenly felt very dizzy. he sat down on a bench trying to take in everything. How could Herobrine still be alive? Who were the other three villains with him? Where were they going to go next?

Alex came running towards the crowd. "Hey, there's a special TV broadcast in a minute!" Everyone ran into the village hall as the screen crackled into to life. There was a woman holding a microphone standing in front of a scene of demolition. All the skyscrapers windows were smashed, smoke was rising from the houses and there wasn't a sign of life.

The news reporter said, "Herobrine has been destroying cities and towns far and wide. I am reporting to you from Axeblade." Alex and Dave gasped. "There has been mass-"

The broadcast cut off for a few seconds before Herobrine's face flashed onto the screen. It filled the TV- nobody knew where he was or what his surrounding were like. The speaker crackled and the whole crowd seemed to catch its breath. Herobrine opened his mouth to speak. "Revenge-will- be- MINE!" Then the broadcast was cut. Everyone was totally gobsmacked after what they had just seen. They all remembered the day when Toby, Herobrine's cover identity terrorized Daint along with the Wither.

Out of nowhere, Lofty teleported beside Steve. Everyone was in too much of a panic to notice an Enderman inside the hall. Alex came over to them. "What's happening?"

'Herobrine is after the Command block. I know where is base is- in the woodlands around a thousand blocks away. I overheard him saying how he was going to use the Command Block to wipe out everything on the face of this planet. The Command block is hidden somewhere deep inside a cave, guarded by the strongest, most terrifying monster in existence- the Warden.'

The Command Block was a specialized block which allowed the user to access limitless Commands which could both devastate and aid a Minecraft world.

Steve filled in the village Elder about all of this. His head was swimming with how ridiculously fast this had all happened. Then Lofty turned up and randomly started rambling about some Command Block. But the Village Elder took it seriously. He said they needed to get moving before

Herobrine could get the Command block. It was like he had encountered it before. The other problem was the Warden. Steve had never heard of it but apparently whoever encountered it never came back to tell the tale. Just to be sure, he quickly crafted up some potions in the brewery, its brand-new brewing stand taking the spotlight.

The village Elder said the Command block in the deep dark, many thousands of blocks away from here. Even Lofty couldn't teleport that far! The only other efficient method of travel was through the Nether. And Steve wasn't looking particularly forward to going back down there. Ever.

******

Chapter 5

Steve gulped. Nervously, he struck the flint and steel together. The portal was ready to go. All they had to do was walk east for a couple hundred blocks and then build another portal back to the Overworld. Every block in the Nether was equal to eight in the Overworld, which meant that they were travelling eight times the distance than if they were in the Overworld.

It was the only way to reach the Command block before Herobrine. Steve stepped into the portal along with, Alex, Lofty and Shadow (he didn't really know why he was bringing his ocelot with but Steve decided to anyways). Plus, he thought he underestimated his small pet cat quite a lot. They all stepped into the portal. All of a sudden, everything slowed to a crawl. Steve stepped into the gunk. They were walking on soul sand, which caused movement to become a lot slower. Patches of blue fire were everywhere and the desolate landscape was littered with bones. The only moving thing there was the skeletons that patrolled their land.

"Oh, this is going to be annoying!" said Steve. "A Soul Sand valley!" He stepped out onto the brownish sand. It sank under his feet. "Come on." said Alex. Shadow, who was having no trouble walking sauntered along, looking longingly at the Nether bones poking out every few paces.

Luckily, the skeletons didn't notice the group apart from a few who decided to teach their kids how to fire a bow.

After many painful hours of walking, they soon reached a ledge facing a beautiful but dangerous crimson forest. 'This is the place!" said Lofty. He teleported down. Lofty didn't feel the most comfortable, preferring to be in the contrasting warped forest surrounded by his kin. He built up the portal, signalling the other to join him. But, just as they were about to climb down, a sword blade flew out from the trees and struck Lofty in the arm. Steve barely saw the glinting object slice through the sizzling air. He cried out as his attacker walked out of the forest. It was Null.

So this is who I saw, thought Steve. Null didn't seem to have a solid form; he was a spirit of darkness. His eyes glowed white just like Herobrine's. They were just as bad as each other. Picking up the flint and steel, he lit the portal. Sword in hand, Steve leapt off the ledge. But it was too late. Null was already gone. "No!" Steve knelt down beside Lofty. He looked weak but gave Steve a thumbs up before flopping down again. Alex handed him a golden apple. He ate it slowly.
"We need to catch up with Null." said Steve. "Alex, you and Shadow stay with Lofty."

"Are you sure Steve? Can you take on the Warden and Null by yourself?" asked Alex worriedly.
"I'll be fine." he replied before jumping into the portal. Steve exited into a dark cavern. Stalagmites and stalactites lined

the ground and ceiling. Running through the cavern, Steve soon approached a peculiar sight.

A strange darkish-blue block had taken over part of the chamber. It glowed softly and was dotted with sculk sensors; it had four thin, blue tentacles growing out of it and growled softly if it felt vibration. The sculk carried on deeper into the cave. The more noise Steve made, the more the sensors growled. He cautiously sneaked on. A sense of foreboding was growing stronger as he ventured further into the territory of the Warden.

Soon Steve reached a dead end. About to turn back, he noticed a little crack in the wall. Steve slid through it, but the ledge he was standing on crumbled. Steve placed down hay bales as he fell to the ground. This absorbed most of the fall damage.

He looked around. He was in some kind of underground ruined city. The Ancient City! He had found it! It was primarily composed of deepslate bricks. Intimidating skulls lined the hallways and the fact that the ancient city was half underwater here reminded Steve of Atlantis. The city had long since been deserted. Eerie soul lanterns were dotted around, illuminating the dusty chests full of ancient wonders, like echo shards. Pools of dirty water were situated in the dilapidated courtyards, possibly the earliest forms of Jacuzzis. Rotting wooden lookout posts were a common sight, most of their roofs crumbled in and gaps in the floor boards. The Sculk continued into the heart of the city, breaking off into veins slithering through the corridors like a serpent.

But the most curious thing of all was the rectangular structure in the middle of the ancient city. It was made of reinforced deepslate, an almost indestructible block. All this while, the infectious sculk encased the ancient city in its gloomy atmosphere. Bone blocks were scattered around the city, adding to the overall spooky feeling the place gave Steve. If the Nether had terrified him, it was nothing compared to this.

Not having the time to explore, Steve ran forwards, looking for Null. His boots clattered on the stone. Suddenly, everything went dark. The sculk sensors howled. Steve couldn't see a thing. He crept forward slowly, walking towards the portal-like structure. If there was one place the Command block would be, it was there. Still no sign of Null, thought Steve. Where was he?

Steve approached the structure. He hadn't seen anything like it before. What was this thing? Veins of sculk crept around it like a snake coiling itself around a victim. Suddenly, a shadow jumped out from behind Steve. "Null!" shouted Steve. He began chasing after Null, running through the dark passages.

Everything went dark again. When everything returned to normal, Null was nowhere to be found. Steve continued looking around. Then a bright beam of light erupted from behind him. Null had the Command block with his head bent over it, secretly typing in a Command. Steve's heart sank. He approached carefully. Just as he was about to leap in with his sword, Steve was thrown back into a crumbling wall. Blue sound rays, flew at him from the darkness, crashing into the wall which immediately gave in.

Steve found himself in pitch black once more. Something was coming. He kept very still and silent. Steve's eyes adjusted to the darkness just in time as something crashed into him. He fell to the floor. His leg was in too much pain; even the diamond armour couldn't protect him completely. He caught a glimpse of Null smashing down on the Command block and teleporting himself away. Then he closed his eyes.

Steve came to lying on the damp cave floor. He was still in the ancient city but he couldn't see the Warden either. What had just happened? He slowly got to his feet. He needed to escape. Steve slowly sneaked back towards his Nether portal. Then he heard a crunch from behind him. It was the Warden.

******

Chapter 6

It was an intimidating beast, standing over two blocks tall. It had frilly ears, listening for vibrations. A set of jaws poked out from its torso, storing the sound waves which it launched at victims. It looked strong enough to knock out an iron golem in one hit. It roared at Steve menacingly, before launching its sound waves at him. Steve rolled out of the way and sliced with his sword. It snapped like a twig as it made contact with the Warden.

Steve was shocked. This was crazy! The Warden almost lazily punched Steve. He staggered back. His armour had many cracks all over it. Steve peppered the Warden with arrows as he ran. He could hear crunching and shuffling behind him. Sound rays flew at him from everywhere. They were deafening. It was like being inside a volcano when it erupted. Where was the portal? Steve suddenly stumbled and he was plunged deep into the arctic water. A blow from the Warden was one thing but the icy water was like a knife piercing through him.

Steve emerged gasping and leant on the outposts which immediately crumbled. He was sure the Warden had heard. Steve ran, headed over towards a glowing purple light source which could have been his portal. But, as he turned a bend, the warden used sonic boom once more and the archway collapsed, blocking off the portal. Steve raised his shield and turned to face the Warden. It hadn't smelled him out yet. Steve picked up a loose pebble and threw it over the wall.

Roaring, the beast stalked off towards the sound. Steve pulled out his pickaxe and mined his way towards the portal. The Warden roared with rage as it realised it had been tricked. Steve hurriedly jumped into the portal, vanishing.

Panting, Steve jumped out into the Nether. Alex and Lofty were waiting for him. "What happened asked Alex. Steve shook his head sadly. "Null got the Command block!" Lofty gasped. This was bad. Shadow mewed serenely. It was pretty obvious she didn't have a clue about what was going on. Suddenly, they heard a rustle from behind them. Herobrine stepped towards them. "Herobrine! How?" Steve asked. He just merely laughed as he was joined by Entity 303 and Deathlord. They were both loyal servants of Herobrine. Entity 303 wielded a large scythe, while Deathlord had a sword.

"Okay, take one each." Steve whispered to Alex and Lofty. "Shadow, run!" he added. Shadow took off as the battle began. Steve battled Herobrine who had only seemed to get stronger. Steve warped behind him and fired an arrow. It went through Herobrine like he wasn't there. He advanced towards Steve. He remembered the last time he had fought his nemesis. It had ended with the loss of his loyal friend.

Meanwhile, Alex was parrying Entity's consistent attacks with her trident. Still, Entity 303 was too fast and dragged his scythe deep into Alex's armour. Alex ate a chorus fruit and teleported up onto a tree. From there, she fired arrow after arrow at him with her crossbow. Entity 303 expertly spun his scythe round and deflected all the arrows. As if he was a frog, Entity leaped up onto the tree which Alex was on. She jumped off just in time as he sliced the tree clean in half.

Lofty was also struggling to keep up with Deathlord who swiped so fast with his sword; he could barely see the attacks coming. On top of that, Deathlord could summon undead mobs like skeletons and zombies. Lofty did his best to punch them away but with no luck.

Steve drank a potion of regeneration. Suddenly the ground around Herobrine started to shake. He summoned in his most powerful weapon: The Chaos Slayer. Herobrine seemed to have a variety of deadly swords and Steve had no idea how he had acquired this one- Null had probably prepared it for him with the Command Block. It was a long, metal sword with purple energy crackling throughout it. Aiming it at Steve, bright bolts of electricity burst out from it. Steve jumped out of the way as it ripped into the ground and exploded in violent sparks. Shields were no good against Herobrine and the only thing you could do was dodge his ferocious attacks. Steve was up against something totally different than anything he had faced before. Steve knew this and had no intention of finding out what happened if he was hit by that lightning bolt.

Knowing they didn't have a chance, Steve, Alex and Lofty regrouped. As if things couldn't get any worse, Null chose that moment to return with the Command block. Presenting it to Herobrine, he also drew out a blade. "We are outnumbered!" said Alex. "What should we do?" Steve said, "Just get to the Command block, then we can teleport away with it. Null, Entity 303 and Deathlord had formed a tight circle around the Command block. Herobrine levitated into the air, with the Chaos Slayer and pointed it at the trio. Steve and Alex ate a golden apple each, but they knew that wouldn't be enough. The blade charged with electricity as the energy formed into a sphere. Steve shielded his eyes as the sphere grew bigger and brighter before flying towards them.

Steve braced himself for impact but he felt nothing. He heard a loud crack and when he opened his eyes, Shadow was lying in front of them, unmoving. "Shadow!" Steve ran forward. Herobrine laughed. Steve was filled with rage. He felt like a firecracker about to go off. And he did.

Red waves were floating out of Steve as if he was emitting his anger. His diamond sword glowed crimson. He felt so powerful! What was going on? Steve flew at Herobrine at light speed, grabbing hold of him and smashing into a wall. An indent was left where Herobrine had crashed into. He fired another energy ball at Steve who deflected it with his sword before him and sent it back at Herobrine. He ducked as it slammed into Deathlord who fell to the floor, jerking suddenly from the overload of electricity.

Herobrine and Steve clashed together, neither of them backing away. Suddenly, Steve felt drained of his power and was easily pushed back by Herobrine. He was dizzy; what had happened? Alex had made a run for the Command block but Null simply clicked something and she froze. She couldn't move.

Noticing this, Steve threw two ender pearls at the same time: one ten blocks left of where he was standing and another at the Command block. He teleported to his left first and all the remaining villains charged at him. A second later, he warped next to the Command block. It had so many buttons and switches; Steve was overwhelmed. He flicked down a random button. Everyone there was thrown back at least five blocks. Scrambling to his feet, Steve made a dash to the Command block along with everyone else.

Lofty picked up Shadow gingerly and teleported to the Command block. Deathlord (who had recovered from his electric overdose) clung onto the Command block as Steve reached it. They all held onto it as Alex teleported them away.

They were back in the Overworld now. Herobrine and his gang had also teleported with them. Herobrine was the first to gather his bearings and zapped everyone away from the Command block with his sword. Laughing mirthlessly, he punched down on a button. Immediately, a mass of zombies spawned in front of Steve and Alex. Herobrine typed in something and he, Null, Entity 303 and Deathlord were all gone in a flash. Now there were the zombies to deal with. They swarmed the small group who were already not at their best.

'I have an idea!' said Lofty telepathically. 'Dig down one block.' Alex and Steve shared a look or bewilderment. What? Regardless, they mined the block beneath them. Lofty placed down a block of obsidian and put an end crystal on top. Activating it, it exploded, obliterating everything around them. Alex and Steve had barely took any damage themselves; digging down had made them blast proof, just like Lofty said.

'Quick!' he shouted. The mobs were still spawning. Following the drill, the three linked arms with Shadow still being carried by Lofty. They teleported back to Daint.

******

Chapter 7

"What happened here?" asked the Village Elder as he examined all of them. "Null-"

"They were too-"

"The Warden-"

"Calm down! Let's hear everything from start to finish." said the Elder. They went inside. Steve started to explain everything from start to finish. "Shadow jumped in front of the shot." said Steve sadly. He handed the village Elder the unmoving feline. He inspected Shadow and said "It's not too bad. She should pull through."

Both Steve and Alex breathed a sigh of relief. They continued narrating the story until the point where they teleported back. "This is bad. Very bad." said the village Elder. "With the Command block, who knows what havoc Herobrine could release into the world? But I do know someone who might be able to help."

The village Elder spread out a crumpled map. Jabbing his finger at the mountain range, he said, "This is where we need to go. There is an outpost there- home to the Pillagers."

"But I thought Villagers and Pillagers were enemies?"Asked Alex. The Pillagers had raided many villages and burned all the houses to ashes. "They are. But I don't think we have much of a choice- they are a worthy force to be reckoned with, even for Herobrine." finished the village Elder. "Prepare for the journey tomorrow. Let's go."

Steve walked back to his house miserably. How could he let Herobrine get the Command block? The mission was an absolute failure. Lofty had been stabbed, Shadow might've been taken out by the Chaos Slayer, the Warden had nearly finished him and they had lost the Command block above all. Steve felt so angry at himself. None of this would've happened if he had made sure Herobrine was gone forever. He should've known Herobrine could just teleport out of the void. Nothing was going right. And Jay's sacrifice... Trying to forget about all of this, Steve just went to bed.

***

The next morning, they set for the mountains. It wasn't really that far away but the perilous peaks and colossal mountains meant that they had to take a detour through the forest. The village Elder had banned teleporting there because the Pillagers probably wouldn't appreciate them popping up right in front of their faces.

Steve, Alex and the Village Elder began the trek to the outpost. Lofty and Shadow had stayed behind to heal from their injuries. It was just them. A few hours later, they reached the outpost. It was surrounded by many pillagers holding crossbows. There were a few empty cages and piles of logs surrounding the main structure. It was made of mossy cobblestone and spruce wood. Illager banners hung on the walls; every outsider knew this was an Illager-only residence. Spying at the Pillagers from the bushes, the Village Elder signalled Steve and Alex to follow him. As soon as they stepped out of the bush, all the pillagers were onto them like flies. While Steve and Alex blocked their arrows, the Elder said, "We come in peace. Herobrine shall destroy both Villagers and Pillagers. We need your help to stop them."

The Pillager general held up a hand. The rest of the Pillagers stopped shooting. The general went inside. He returned a few minutes later with the leader of the clan. He had an eye patch over one eye and a wooden leg. The raid captain had an ominous banner on his back, the same one on the wall. He grunted at the village Elder, telling him to come inside. The rest of the Pillagers kept an eye on Steve and Alex with their crossbows loaded. It was quite awkward.

Soon the Village Elder came out accompanied by the raid captain. Somehow he had wangled a deal. They had made a truce. Villagers and Pillagers united to stop Herobrine!

******

Chapter 8

The raid captain's name was John. He was responsible for many village raids, including Daint. Back around half a century ago, the Pillagers had invaded Daint when John's grandfather was the raid captain. They had reached a compromise that when Herobrine had been defeated, they would become enemies once more. Having no other choice, the village Elder gave in.

John, along with all the other Pillagers, walked to Daint, following Steve and Alex. John narrowed his eyes at all the houses he would love to raid and villagers he would love to attack. John had told them that more Illagers would be coming to help; Vindicators, Evokers and Ravagers. Steve just hoped they weren't planning one big raid. But the village Elder had trusted John so Steve couldn't help but trust him either. More than anything, Steve was surprised the Pillagers were civilised enough to do their own laundry.

All the Pillagers had caused a big stir in the village. Most of the Villagers were hiding in their houses while the Iron golem was advancing towards the party. The village Elder held up his hand. The iron golem stopped in his tracks but was still blowing out puffs of steam. It looked like he had run into these Pillagers before.

"It is fine. They're on our side this time." said the Elder. "They won't attack us!" Soon the whole village was warming towards their Pillager cousins. Still, no one offered a room to them or give them a proper job. It was no wonder villagers didn't trust Pillagers after their rocky history.

In the few weeks after the Pillagers arrived, nothing big happened. There were still reports of Herobrine attacking towns and cities but there were no nasty run-ins for a while. In this time, Steve had recruited a group of Enderman led by Lofty. Shadow had also got into the action, gathering her own cat army who really didn't do much apart from nose at tins of fish wherever they went. Shadow herself had more or less healed from her injury, even though she still had a scar from where the energy ball had hit her.

Steve tried to keep her away from danger as much as he could these days which is why he didn't bring her along on his next exploit (still, he was utterly grateful to her). John had recommended moving over to the woodland mansion where the rest of the Illagers resided.

Lofty, with his geographical knowledge, pointed out that Herobrine's base wouldn't be too far away. It was a big decision: they wouldn't be coming back to Daint for at least a good few months. However, Steve knew it would be best to move over, as close as Herobrine's base as they could. John had spoken to the village Elder about this- he had agreed to move out. Lofty and all the other Enderman had been helping out moving things to the mansion. It was only essentials like food, armour, weapons and other utilities as such. Steve, Alex, the Village Elder, Shadow and all the Pillagers and Enderman were going to the mansion. Dave, the lumberjack who Steve had rescued from the End, was also coming along, as he wanted his daughter's company. Steve, not wanting to bring along half of the village with him, didn't allow anyone else to come along with him. (Though Shadow was rather gutted that she and her cat friends couldn't come along.) Steve wanted to keep her safe after their last little adventure together.

Steve looked sadly at the village. He wasn't coming back here anytime soon. Defeating Herobrine was what mattered. Speaking of Herobrine, Steve realised he still had the Command block and could be typing a Command that would blow up half the world at this moment. He really hoped that wasn't the case. Within a day, the Enderman had teleported all of their stuff to the woodland mansion. It was time for Steve and everyone else to go. Teleporting with an Enderman each, everyone had soon safely reached the mansion. Their new home.

******

Chapter 9

The mansion was massive. It was a large, rectangular build several stories high. Its flat roofs housed many unwelcoming mobs and a convenient place to sunbath (not that the zombies or skeletons needed it.)

It was plonked right in the middle of woodland of dark oak. Giant mushrooms and huge dark oak trees surrounded it. Its entrance was covered with leafs and thorns, leaving Steve to wonder how anyone actually got in. The inside of the mansion was even more impressive than the outside. It was dimly lit, causing a creepy effect. The panelled floor was covered in a neat array of red and white carpet, muffling the footsteps of the vindicator guards. The maze-like layout of the place meant that there were many winding passages, leading into darkness. The mansion was filled with a huge variety of rooms. Large beds sat in furnished suites contradicted by the dark dungeons that were littered by bones. Libraries held many books; mainly about battle strategies and how to take over villages. Imposing Illager mosaics decorated the walls along with bracketed torches. Around every bend, there were always Illager to be found. Whether it was the stern vindicators with sharp iron axes or the powerful evokers in their black and yellow robes, there was never a shortage of Illagers.

Still, Steve didn't think it would be enough to face Herobrine and his gang. One evening at dinner, he said, "Why can't you recruit other Pillager clans?" John spat half a carrot out of his mouth. "Why don't we recruit other clans? The other Pillagers are no less than vermin. Why should we follow the orders of the other raid captains when we have a mansion full of our own Illagers?" Steve reminded himself no to be so nosy next time.

Lofty and the other Enderman preferred to stay out of everyone's way which is why no one really saw them much. Steve and Alex had no intention of taking lead and left the Village Elder and John to work out the battle plan while they explored the mansion. They had found plenty of loot chests filled with enchanted iron axes but let them be to stay on the Vindicator's good side. As they explored the mansion, Steve and Alex learned new things about the Illagers. The Evokers had a very unique battle style, summoning vexes who flew around the victim, diving in for their attacks. They dropped the Totem of Undying, which made Steve wonder why he had ever gone on a quest to the jungle in the first place while he couldn't have stopped by and picked up a couple of totems from here. Oh well.

Of course, as the Illagers were letting them live in the mansion, they had to earn their stay. Mucking out the Ravager stables was one of their daily chores. The Ravagers were like Iron Golems for Illagers. Oddly resembling a bull, the ravagers had spiky horns coming out of their huge heads and tough, leathery skin. They walked on all fours, slowly plodding along without a care in the world (apart from ramming into trees). As they munched on sweet berries all day, cleaning their dung was no treat.

Steve and Alex had Ravager riding lessons where they were each given a Ravager to ride. Steve named his Rocksteady. He was the biggest Ravager in the herd who had no worries throwing Steve off his back like shaking away a fly. But soon Alex and Steve both mastered the art of riding and were riding their Ravagers out into the forests like walking a dog.

Not much news had reached anyone in the mansion. Still, John and the Village Elder thought it was the right time to act. Lowly Vindicators were sent out on spy missions daily, informing John of Herobrine's plans. According to one young Illager the Command block was heavily guarded by Herobrine's servants. There was no way to get to it. Unless...

******

Chapter 10

This is a really bad idea you know!" said Alex as she and Steve snuck up to Herobrine's base. The plan was to use Alex as bait- which she wasn't too happy about- to lure away Herobrine's cronies so Steve could get the Command block. And from there it would be child's play.

Steve had to say that Herobrine's base was impressive. It was open-planned, with obsidian walls four blocks high. The courtyard grounds were made of tinted black glass. Steve couldn't see what was under it. The actual base was obviously created using the Command block. It was massive, made of a mix of strong blocks: bedrock pillars (obtained using Commands), a complex obsidian framework and more tinted black glass. Glowstone was dotted around the base and Steve could just make out thin lines of redstone- probably for a secret passage. Underground, Steve could hear many pistons at work and loud explosions. Herobrine was testing something. Something big.

Although the base had so many hiding spots, the Command block was sitting in the middle of the courtyard. Nothing was guarding it. "Wow!" whispered Steve. Alex nudged him to remind him of why they had come. "Oh, right." said Steve. "Go for it!" Alex crept forward cautiously. Something was off. Why was there no one in sight? Maybe it was a trap...

Alex continued forward and dropped into the courtyard. Her boots made a loud ring as they came in contact with the glass. Freezing, she looked around. Nothing happened. It was safe. Alex waved at Steve to let him know it was safe. A few seconds later, he had rejoined with Alex. He stepped towards the Command block. But, as Steve reached out to grab it, the floor fell away beneath him and Alex.

"Aaaaaaah!" they both screamed as they hurtled down in to the dark. Thump! They had landed on something very, very hard. Rubbing his head, Steve looked around. He could see a circle of daylight above him. Herobrine was standing at the edge of the floor. "HA!" he declared with glee. "I've been waiting for this!" He pressed a button on the Command block. Suddenly, something growled at them from the darkness.

Steve placed down a torch. His and Alex's eyes' nearly popped out of their sockets. Standing in front of them was a wither skeleton fully kitted out in enchanted diamond armour holding a diamond sword. Herobrine had summoned in this abomination through Commands. The pair hadn't bought their best armour for this situation. The hatch above Steve and Alex closed, leaving them to fight the wither skeleton. It ran at them with increased speed, landing a hit on Alex. She was thrown back into the bedrock wall, starting to wither away.

Steve shoved a bucket of milk towards her to cure Alex while he took on the skeleton. Each hit he landed on the skeleton seemed to do nothing. On the other hand, his armour had been pierced through and he had some deep cuts under his shirt. On top of that, he had the wither effect like Alex. However, he just didn't seem to get the opportunity to drink a bucket of milk to get rid of the annoying but lethal side effect.

The diamond sword also seemed to do much more damage than usual- it was probably enchanted with some form of sharpness. His shield splintered as he blocked another attack. It had cracked but it was still intact. Steve lashed out with a kick. It sent the skeleton stumbling backwards. Steve leapt towards it and thrust with his axe. The sharp end ripped through the armour, lodging itself deep into the skeleton. It seemed surprised for a second before falling to the floor. Steve picked up its diamond sword which was a good replacement for his iron axe. Alex had recovered and was studying the walls of the pit to see if there was any way out. They obviously couldn't break their way out- bedrock was indestructible.

"Steve, do you have a water bucket by any chance?" Alex asked. Steve handed his over without any question. She placed down the water on the wall which flowed down to the floor. She swam up the column of water, quickly picking up the water and placing it down a few blocks higher each time as she climbed up.

"Ok, that's smart!" admitted Steve as he followed Alex back up to freedom. They mined the hatch and breathed in the cool night air. There was no one around. Both Herobrine and the Command block were gone. They peered down the hole they had just climbed up. It was deep. Having no intention of exploring Herobrine's base for the Command block, Steve and Alex walked back to the mansion. It was easy enough to find because it glowed like a beacon in the dark, with the windows reflecting all the light from the torches. Steve and Alex headed back through the forest. Still, the feeling of unease never left Steve. It was like being back in the forest with Lofty but without a trusty Enderman like him to protect them.

Steve had shaken off the feeling of unease by the time they had reached the concealed mansion entrance. Steve and Alex walked back inside to fill in the Village Elder about their quest. But, little did they know, Null had been watching them all along. Smirking, he turned back to Herobrine's base. It was time.

***

Steve woke up in the middle of the night. He didn't know what had woken him. He was in his comfortable double bed in one of the King suites. Steve thought he had heard someone talking. He strained his ears but everything was silent. Still, Steve climbed out of bed and walked out of his room onto the dark corridors. Alex's room was right next to his. He checked on her but everything seemed to be ok.

Suddenly, he smelt something. The smell of something burning. Steve ran down the corridor. Where was that smell coming from? Just as he was thinking that, the Village Elder ran towards him. "Steve! Run! Herobrine knows we're here!" he shouted. A scream sounded throughout the mansion. Steve looked behind him. The corridor was up in flames. He ran past the village Elder, up onto the roof. Herobrine and his gang was standing there. Deathlord was setting the mansion on fire while Entity 303 was loading up a redstone machine with TNT. IT was a TNT cannon! Noticing Steve, he flicked the lever. TNT came flying at him. He leapt out of the way as the explosive blew its way open into the plotting room. Steve jumped in through the shattered glass as Entity 303 launched more TNT at the mansion.

The hallways were filled with panicking Illagers running away from either the white- hot flames or the TNT being launched at them.

Steve had some stuff he needed to get from his room but he knew there was no time for that. He had lost the Village Elder in this mess but hoped John and the other Pillagers would protect him. Steve wished Lofty was around but he and the other Enderman didn't live in the mansion. Now it was complete chaos. Steve was blown down the stair by TNT and was just about to be crushed by a burning oak plank that was falling above him when the floor crumbled to ashes from the fire. He fell into the library an Evoker was hiding. Steve reached out to help him but yet another TNT exploded in front of him. Herobrine had summoned a TNT rain!

Steve then remembered Rocksteady. He needed to find him and also get as low as possible. A horde of zombies poured into the mansion, summoned by Deathlord. Steve took a diversion and ran down a narrow archway. The archway led to some cells. Inside, were small pixie- like blue creatures. These were Allay. They could be used to collect any object in their arms. Steve flicked the lever and freed them all. Three zombies walked in after him. Steve mined into the floor, blocking of the zombies. He eventually dug into another bedroom. It was just like his, but inverted. He was on the other side of the mansion now.

Steve was about to run out of the door but flaming wood collapsed over his exit. "No!" Steve punched the glass windows as hard as he could. Soon they broke. Steve looked down. It was a long way to jump. Whelp. He had no other choice. Taking one look back at the room, Steve leapt out into the night.

******

Chapter 11

He was falling. Cool night air rushed past him. Steve pulled out a ladder and placed it down on the dark oak wall. Grabbing on with one hand, Steve caught his breath before falling the rest of the way. Splash! He had landed in a small stream. Then he remembered something he thought had been missing. Alex! Where was she? Steve sprinted around the mansion until he reached the entrance. This was stupid, but he needed to find Alex. Steve lingered before the door hesitantly. He was safe out here... Steve shook his head. He was going to save them. He pushed through the wall of brambles into the inferno.

"ALEX! Where are you?" Steve cried. There weren't as many Illagers running around now but Alex was still in there. And what about John and the Village Elder? While everyone else ran down the stairs, Steve bolted back into the mansion. He went back to Alex's bedroom but it was half blown up and starting to catch on fire. Alex wasn't there. Nor could he find any familiar Illagers.

Suddenly, a dark shadow loomed over Steve. Herobrine was levitating in mid- air, the Chaos Slayer charged with electricity. Knowing, there was no time to fight, Steve ran for his life. Energy balls ricocheted off the walls, singing the wax paintings that were already melting in the heat.

Steve took many twists and turns, hoping to shake off Herobrine. Just as Steve thought he had lost him, a TNT landed in front of him. He was blown back into the glass window which exploded into glimmering crystals. Steve slid to the edge of the roof, grabbing on. The canopy below him was all that stood between him and solid, hard ground. Even with all his might, Steve just couldn't pull himself up. The overhang was already creaking ominously. Steve desperately screamed for help. The canopy below him was now a mixture of burned wood and flaming leaves. It couldn't end like this. Steve finally let go as the last TNT fell on the roof. BOOOOM!

***

Steve opened his eyes. He was staring at blackened trees with no leaves. The grand forest had been scorched to a pile charred wood. As for the mansion, there wasn't much left of it. Almost all the wood had been burned and embers were still glowing brightly from piles of debris. Steve had fallen quite a distance. It was now early morning and Herobrine was gone. And so was everyone else.

Steve dug around in the rubble for life. He still didn't know what had happened to Alex, the Village Elder, Dave, John and the others. Amongst many other things, he found ripped banners, singed maps and chipped iron axes.

Suddenly, Steve heard a grunting noise coming from the forest. Rocksteady hobbled through the trees and fell on his knees. "Rocksteady!" Steve shouted, running towards his faithful Ravager. Rocksteady was injured. One of his horns had snapped off and his tough skin was burned. He was also coughing and wheezing from the overdose of smoke last night. The stables must have caught fire, thought Steve. He brought Rocksteady some sweet berries to munch on while he bandaged the base of his horn and washed him down with water. No other Ravagers were with him and Steve could tell from the look in Rocksteady's eyes that none of the others had made it.

Steve continued searching. "Steve! Help!" someone called out hoarsely. He recognized the voice. It was Dave. He was trapped under a pile of cobblestone. One by one, Steve unburied Dave and helped him to his feet. "Thank you." he said quietly before dropping down like Rocksteady. "Hey, take it easy," said Steve. "Here." He handed Dave his water bottle. He gulped it all down like a thirsty camel in the desert.

"Do you know where Alex and the other are? Dave asked. Steve shook his head sadly. "It was all my fault." he whispered. Dave tried to console him. "It's not your fault!" he said. "How could you have known Herobrine knows where we live?" Steve knew Dave was right. Still, he should have found Alex and the others.

"You're right," he said reluctantly. "But we have to go before Herobrine and the others come back. Steve mounted Rocksteady and nudged him gently. He broke into a steady plod as Dave jumped on.

"So, where to?" asked Dave.

"I don't know. Maybe back to Daint?" he replied even though he knew it was not a good idea. What was the point of going back there? It wouldn't help them defeat Herobrine. At least they would be safe there. No, thought Steve. I have to end what I started.

So Steve, Dave and Rocksteady's adventure began together, travelling lands far and wide in search of help. Steve grew increasingly frustrated as the time passed by because no one seemed to know anything about how to defeat Herobrine. They couldn't get the Command block so Steve had to think of other ways of defeating Herobrine. But one night, it happened.

They were trekking up a high mountain. It was snowing hard and Rocksteady had a severe cold. He was slowly dragging himself along the rocky peaks with Dave and Steve supporting him. The weather was getting worse. Steve and Dave had no winter gear so needed shelter fast. Soon it began snowing so much Steve couldn't see his own hand in front of his face. Dave was shivering and Rocksteady was coughing loudly. When he coughed, his body shook like he was in an earthquake. Steve was about to call it a day when he saw a light up ahead. A warm, yellow light shone through all the fog and snow. "Hello?" Steve called out, shielding himself from the snowflakes. By now, it was impossible to see. Steve edged forward with his hand held out in front of him. His hand soon hit something hard. It was wood. Steve shuffled along until he reached a door. He burst inside and welcomed the wave of heat. A second later, Dave and Rocksteady joined him. (The doorway was quite big.)

Steve crashed in front of the fire, savouring the warmth. He was joined by a clandestine figure clad in winter clothes. He was completely covered, even his eyes. He was wearing sunglasses even though it was below freezing outside. He pulled down his muffler and said, "What brings you here, traveller?"

Steve said, "We need help to defeat Herobrine." Steve knew that this was a random person's house he had barged into and might not be looking to do him any favours. Still, he needed help.

"Please, have a seat and let's discuss your predicament." he said. Steve sat down in an old leather armchair. Dave and Rocksteady were huddled by the fire, not noticing the stranger. "Who are you?" Steve questioned. The stranger ignored Steve and continued talking. "Tell me your story." Steve narrated everything from start to finish. The man looked unimpressed. "Herobrine is not to be messed with." he said shortly. "But I do know how you can destroy the Command block..."

******

Chapter 12

Alex woke up to an Evoker shaking her awake. She groaned and pushed herself up. She had a faint memory of the mansion burning down and TNT exploding all around her. Alex looked around at her surroundings. She was in a glade, lying on damp soil. Lofty popped up behind the Evoker. He gave Alex a little wave. She waved back and stood up. There was no one else around.

"Where am I?" she asked. The Evoker, who was merely a child, said, "Lofty teleported us here after the accident at the mansion. I was asleep when the fire broke out. I was trapped then Lofty and the other Enderman came. They saved me. After the wildfire, we went back to find survivors. And we found you. But everyone else was gone. All the Illagers and your friends. I'm sorry." Alex boiled with rage. She had seen Herobrine summon in a TNT rain and burn the mansion down with her own eyes. Alex wanted to tell the young Evoker but he was probably already in shock from losing the rest of the Illagers.

'We're in the Lush Forests.' Lofty had mastered the art of telepathy. Alex put her hands on her hips and walked around. Where was Steve? Was everyone else safe? What would they do now? A million questions buzzed in her head.

She needed a plan, and now. "Let's find Steve and the others. Come on!" Alex, Lofty and the young Evoker, who was called Xenos, set off to find the others. Steve, Dave, the village Elder, John; they all had to be found. Alex learned a lot more about Xenos as they searched for their lost friends. He was only a couple of centuries old and was still learning how to control his powers. The only thing he seemed to be able to do was summon a vex the size of a housefly. Xenos was the last of the Evokers. He wore black and yellow robes that were way too long for him and always had a few of his housefly- sized vexes around to protect him. Vexes were small, devilish, winged angels. They could go through blocks to attack a player and had tiny iron swords. Just like Steve, Alex was becoming angrier each day that she couldn't find anyone. Maybe it was for nothing; they were all gone.

"AAARRGHH!" Herobrine screamed as he threw down the ancient book. "NO!" Null came running into the room, alarmed and frightened at seeing his master like this. "What happened?" he said. Herobrine maintained his tone and spoke. "The Command block has a weakness. With the Ender Axe, anyone could destroy the Command block including me. Null silently listened. The very thought of something that could destroy anything, even Herobrine, scared him to the bones (even though he didn't have any). "But I have a plan to finish Steve and the rest- if they even survived." He rubbed his hands together. Steve had met his match.

***

"So, to destroy the Command block, you need something very special." said the stranger. Steve listened carefully. "The book of the Ancients. This will tell you how to destroy the Command block. You can find it in the ancient city." It's hidden in one of the underground chests. Steve nearly spat out his tea. He had to go back there? He didn't even know if he could trust this guy! "Then, you can make the Ender Axe."

Right, I quit, thought Steve. First, he needed the luck to find the Book of the Ancients. Then, he had to risk his life to get whatever it told him to. Steve really wanted to destroy the Command block but this? He couldn't do it. "Guys, we're going." he said to Dave and Rocksteady as he walked towards the door. Steve hadn't even listened to whatever other nonsense the strange man was telling him. He immediately began to regret his decision as he stepped into a cold blast of icy wind. Dave and Rocksteady followed him out. They couldn't care less about what Steve had been talking about. "Steve, both me and Rocksteady are really tired. Can't we just stay for the night?" pleaded Dave. Steve shook his head. We'll find shelter somewhere else. Dave and Rocksteady reluctantly dragged themselves towards Steve. They had no option but to keep searching.

Something had been niggling Steve for a while. Suddenly, his blood ran cold. His heart seemed like it was trying to bounce out of his ribcage. Steve turned around. And there, standing in place of the man, was Herobrine. "I've been watching you for a long time," he said. "You want to destroy the Command block? Well, you're free to do so." And with that he pulled out his demonic chaos slayer, and pointed at Steve. Purple wisps of energy flew at Steve, passing through him like a ghost. Steve fell to the snow- covered floor. Herobrine laughed. Dave leapt at him with his axe but it was too late. Herobrine was gone.

"Steve! Wake up!" Steve didn't respond. Dave slapped him a few times. His heart was still beating so he was clearly alive. Rocksteady licked Steve's ear with his leathery tongue. Steve turned over and opened his eyes. "That's gross!"He said, backing away from the Ravager. Dave laughed. Steve, Dave and Rocksteady progressed down the mountain. Steve was still working out what had happened last night. If the man had been Herobrine, then there was no way he was telling the truth about finding the book. But then again, he had nothing to lose by giving away the secret to destroying the Command block. Herobrine knew there was no chance of them getting the item. Steve also wondered why Herobrine couldn't have just taken him down without ever saying a word. He certainly had a very weird way of doing things.

Dave was secretly worried. He had been wondering why Herobrine couldn't have just spiked his tea with something or rigged a TNT trap. This made him all the more unpredictable. Still, he had attacked Steve. Steve had told him about the book. Dave also though there was very little chance of getting them. He had never been in the Deep Dark before. (Dave had been in the End before but preferred not to talk about that).

Steve was casually walking along when he started sinking into the snow. His face was frozen with fear as he disappeared. Dave was jolted out of his thoughts. He reached into the powdered snow to save Steve but the cold was too painful. He quickly withdrew his fingers. He could see a vague human figure sinking deeper into the translucent ice. Steve was frantically trying to swim out of the numbing snow. Dave thrust his hand into the snow again and found Steve's arm. He pulled with all his might. Rocksteady furiously shovelled the snow out with his horns. Steve's head was out but his legs were still n the snow. "Pull!" Dave said as he finally dragged Steve out of the death trap.

The three fell to the floor and caught their breath. However, they didn't have much time to rest because Steve was shivering. A few minutes later, he was huddled next to a warm fire. "I-I th-ink I st-stepped on pow-powdered sn-snow," he stuttered. Dave handed him some tender chicken that he had cooked over the fire. Steve munched on it gratefully. Dave waited until Steve had finished and said, "We need to work out our next move. We have three choices: go back to Daint, which won't really help, look for Alex, John and the Village Elder or find the book." Rocksteady growled. Even he didn't like the idea of questing in the deep dark. Steve sighed. He knew what had to be done. Herobrine could not be trusted, but it was the only logical option. "Let's go find the book, make the Ender Axe, and finish this once and for all."

******

Chapter 13

Herobrine went back to his base in triumph. Everything was going as planned so far. However, Herobrine had a dark secret. He lived off the Command block, which gave him life essence. Herobrine needed to be near the Command block to survive. He had barely pulled himself together to live long enough to find the Command block. So, if the Command block was destroyed, then it was the end of Herobrine too. Herobrine knew this, so kept the Command block with him at all times. Everything was coming together.

"This is it." said Steve. He, Dave and Rocksteady were in the Nether. They had come through via the same portal they used to get to the Command block. Dave had never been in the Nether before and was awed, just as Steve had been. Dave was soaking in the unique environment. "This is marvellous!" he breathed. Steve put his hands on his hips and surveyed their surroundings. He was back in the soul sand valley.

Apart from a few skeletons, there was no one. "Okay," said Steve. "Follow me!" Steve roughly remembered the route to the portal, using large bones poking out of the sand as landmarks. Rocksteady wasn't having a good time; he kept sinking knee-deep in the sand because of his immense weight. Still, he was good for scaring off any skeletons following them. Rocksteady was very afraid of the fire- he hadn't forgotten the incident at the mansion. It's strange, thought Steve. Rocksteady and I are meant to be enemies but here he is saving my life every few seconds!

Riding him would be too slow, so Dave and Steve had to stick to walking. Dave, who was not particularly young, was having a hard time. Every few minutes, he called a halt. They rested up for up to half an hour before being chased off by skeletons. It went on like this until they finally reached the crimson forest. "This is the spot where it happened." said Steve. Steve jumped down off the ledge. He was careful enough to make sure there was no one hiding in the forest. There was no one apart from a few grazing hoglins.

The portal was still activated. Steve signalled Dave and Rocksteady to join him. "Be very careful!" he whispered. They went in the portal one by one, Steve first. Dave and Rocksteady joined him. Steve checked that the other two had got through before continuing on into the deep dark. "Amazing!" said Dave. He had never seen an ancient city, either. "Shhh!" hissed Steve. "Don't make a sound." But it was easier said than done. It was very dark and both Dave and Rocksteady were having trouble navigating. Unlike Steve, they weren't experienced adventurers. Dave kept slipping on rocks while Rocksteady's heavy feet were crunching away on the sculk. Steve sighed. Why had he decided to bring them? He was more used to working with people his level, like Alex. Not a half a ton Ravager and a lumberjack.

Now they needed to find the book of the ancients and get out. Without triggering the Warden. The book was supposedly under the city, so they had to find a good place to get down. Dave and Rocksteady cowered behind Steve as he boldly led the way forward. Fast, but quiet. Steve was starting to recognise some features like the look out posts and the large rectangular structure in the middle. The ancient city had so many secrets. First it had the Command block, now some hidden book. Steve was worried that someone might've been hiding there like Null the last time. Only time would tell if this was a trap.

The book of the ancients could have been in a chest, but Herobrine said it was under the city (if it was possible to go any deeper, that is). Suddenly, Dave accidentally dislodged a floor tile. It rolled down the steps. The sound of rock smashing against rock echoed throughout the deep dark. It left a ringing sound in Steve's head. One of the sculk sensors went off and everything went pitch black. "What's happening?" asked a petrified Dave. Rocksteady was nervously pawing the cave floor. "Don't move a muscle!" Steve said. They all froze. Within moments, the darkness was gone and everything was back to normal. Steve made sure they were all very quiet after that. Apparently, there was some hidden redstone room under the city. The book was probably in there. But how would they get down without alerting the Warden?

"Walk on the wool," Steve said. The wool in the exposed corridors soaked in the sound of their footsteps so they could mover quicker. Steve had decided to go to the large structure in the middle of the city. The Command block had been there, so the book might've been there too. On the way, Steve saw many chests in the eroded city chambers. He really wanted to see what was inside them but he had to find the Book of the Ancients first. Plus, it could summon in the Warden.

Luckily, they reached the centre of the city without any issues. Now to get into the redstone room. There must have been some way other than digging down and setting of the sculk shriekers. Just then, Dave shouted, "I've found something!" Steve ran over. Dave had found a wooden trapdoor. It was incongruous down so deep. This made Steve immediately suspicious. The trapdoor looked a bit fishy. Steve was about to walk away and ignore it but Dave said, "I hear something!" Steve put his ear to the trapdoor. There was some very faint, nearly inaudible whispering. This was too big to miss. They had to go down. "I'll go down while you two stay up here. The book could be down here."

Steve carefully lowered himself down. There could be anything down there. Rocksteady tried to follow his master down but the gap was too small for him. Steve dropped into a tiny space amongst the bedrock. The wool under the ladder softened his fall. He looked around in the small chamber. There were bizarre redstone machines surrounding him, all of them protected by glass. There were redstone lamps, pistons and other redstone contraptions. It was amazing. Someone had been experimenting down here, just like in

Herobrine's base with the TNT cannon. Steve looked around. There was no book. But there was a small, dusty chest tucked away in the corner. Steve walked towards it.

Opening it with a creak, he rummaged through the contents. There were mainly just bits of redstone and things like that. but at the very bottom, there was an aged, leather-bound book. Steve grabbed it and blew the many layers of dust of the ancient book. "I've got it!" he shouted up to Dave and Rocksteady. He flipped open the first page. It was blank. "What?!" he exclaimed. A shrill laugh echoed through the ancient city. Suddenly, Dave screamed from above. "Dave!" Steve said. He ran towards the ladder but iron bars closed around him. He heard a roar and a rumble from above. The Warden.

Herobrine was standing at the top of the trap door. It was a trap after all. He was joined by Null, Entity 303 and Deathlord. "What did you do to Dave and Rocksteady?" Steve asked furiously. How could he have believed Herobrine? "I don't know," he snarled. "You can ask the Warden that. Steve gasped. If he had barely survived, then his friends would last about five seconds. He heard some faint shouting and crunching from above. The Warden was chasing Dave and Rocksteady but didn't seem to mind the four creatures standing above Steve. Steve tried snapping the iron bars with his hands. It didn't work. He grabbed his pickaxe. But it was too late. Herobrine laughed. Steve was about to meet his end.

Chapter 14

"Great!" said Alex. "Try again!" Xenos, Lofty and her were stopping by in the desert for a bit of training. They had had no luck finding anyone and Alex was starting to lose hope. Xenos was practising his fang attack. The stone columns that rose out of the ground were shorter than a tree stump and it took all of Xenos's energy to produce. Alex had him use the attack on her but she merely felt it scrape against her shin. Not wanting to disappoint him, she pretended it hurt and she hopped around in faked agony. Xenos, however, wasn't fooled. He wasn't going to stop until his fangs were powerful enough to uproot a tree, like adult Evokers. 'Maybe you haven't unlocked your full potential yet.' Lofty suggested. Xenos looked down sadly.

"Guys, it's late. We should sleep." Alex said. They made camp underground, safe from any mobs. Alex lay in her bed, wide awake. By the sound of Xenos's breathing, he was asleep. Lofty had gone out to explore the desert a bit as he didn't need sleep. Alex couldn't sleep either. She was very worried about her father, Steve and the Village Elder. Maybe they really had gone. But Alex wasn't going to believe that. They were all out there somewhere. She would find them. They just had to keep searching. Alex last waking thought was how Steve was doing...

The blistering sun shone down low on the desert. Lofty woke his companions up bright and early. He had spotted something last night not too far from here and wanted to investigate it. He prodded Alex and Xenos out of bed and told them to follow him. Lofty took them to the top of a hill. From there, they could see a village. It was nothing like Daint; much smaller and quieter. He thought it was a good idea to check it out. Alex slid down the hill and walked towards the village. There was something strange about it: the place was too quiet. Back in Daint, there had been plenty of noises and the sound of all the people walking about and the children playing.

Here, there was a deathly silence. No one was around. The sandstone structures were part eroded and dusty cobwebs were littered around the village. It looked very old and all the houses were falling apart. The well had long since run dry and the cracked windows were stained with grime over the years. The farm bore no ripe vegetables; all of them were shrivelled due to the lack of water. The hay bale stacks were dried brown straw. Nothing was alive. It was like a ghost town. Alex immediately sensed something wrong. She walked into the village. *What happened here?*, she thought.

She poked here head inside a damaged sandstone house. The bed was covered in dirt and had a broken leg. The cracked stairs had missing tiles. The windows were smashed in and the chest's lid was bent with its contents randomly scattered on the floor. And staring at Alex was a zombified villager. They were villagers who had been attacked by regular zombies that turned them into zombie villager. Alex didn't want to hurt it but the zombie was intent on attacking her. She slowly lured it out and it started burning in the sunlight. Sadly, there was nothing she could do to help it. The rest of the houses were just like the first. Lofty and Xenos were poking around the houses, confused. It was an abandoned village.

They found many more zombies inside the houses, sheltering from the scorching sun. Strangely, there was no iron golem. There was nothing. Lofty had seen cases like this before. It happened when there was huge zombie attack or some other serious event which made the villagers move out many years ago. In this case, the zombies were responsible. A perfectly good village lost. Not an ideal place to live in. Alex decided to see what was in the chests. It was mainly rotten food and junk that no one needed.

This way, the three explored all the buildings. All that was left was the blacksmiths.

It was just as ruined as the rest. The cracked sandstone walls had a high chance of collapsing and letting the lava below the furnaces to flow out. The door was nowhere to be seen- it had been smashed off its hinges. Splinters of wood still remained as evidence. The little table inside where the blacksmith worked had been ripped in two. Snapped chair legs littered the faded oak floor. Cobwebs hung around the room like clouds hanging in the sky. Alex proceeded inside, careful of any more attackers. There was a dusty, wooden chest in the corner with a parchment hanging out of it. It looked fairly new. She dragged it out of the chest, careful not to rip it.

Alex opened the paper up and blew the dust off it. It read:

The Temple of Darkness will greet you with despair,

The hidden map will lead you there,

Traveller, do take care,

Venture inside if you dare.

"What is that supposed to mean?" asked Xenos.

'If you want, we can go there.' Lofty said. 'it might help us find the others.' Alex and Xenos agreed. They would go to the Temple of Darkness. (Alex didn't exactly know why they were going but it sounded like a good idea to go.) Lofty said that the Temple was somewhere in the Nether but he had no idea where. The note had said there was a map hidden somewhere close by so they started to look around. There was no map amongst the rotting furniture. There was nothing. Finally, Lofty wrenched open the weak floor planks. Underneath, there was nothing but a lot of dust. And a map. Unlike the note, it was yellowing with age and the writing was very faint. It was barely readable. Alex unfolded the parchment and had a look at the map. It was a detailed paper version of the Nether. The ink had long since dried out but Alex could read the map properly. They had to enter the Nether at the specific coordinates to reach the Temple. Lofty took the map and looked at it. This was what they needed to get to the temple. As Lofty said, it could give them clues as to where the others were. So they decided to spend the night in the village and set off to the Nether in the morning.

After clearing out a house of cobwebs and mobs, the three went to sleep. They woke up at the crack of dawn, ready to go. On the other side of the parchment, there was a path towards the coordinates. They settled on following that path towards the Nether. Within a few hours of travelling, the little group reached a marsh. It was thick with vegetation and its muddy trees grew out of a knee-deep swamp. Lofty shuddered looking at the water. Like all other Enderman, he couldn't bear it. Instead, Lofty said he would meet the other two on the other side of the marsh.

Alex and Xenos began their wade through the bog. The cold water trickled into Alex's boots and soaked through Xenos's robes. They slowly felt their boots sinking into the muck. Little orange frogs hopped around and the muddy mangrove roots tripped them up as they navigated through the swamp. At long last, they saw fresh grass ahead of them. Alex breathed a sigh of relief as she saw Lofty waving at them. She went to him. Lofty gave Alex the fourteen pieces of obsidian to make the portal. Alex lit it with her flint and steel. They were going in. The three appeared to be in the Nether Wastes. It was a barren biome composed of Netherrack. Lava crawled along its surface and mobs were everywhere. Xenos was terrified. He tried to sneak back through the portal but Lofty dragged him back. In the distance, there was an obscure structure. "Hey, is that the temple?"Asked Alex. Lofty nodded.

As they got closer, the details of the temple became clearer. It was built out of blackstone and Nether bricks. Lava streamed down its walls and Wither skeleton skulls decorated the outside. "It looks more like a prison than a temple." Xenos commented. The three walked over to the temple. Suddenly, and arrow flew at them. Lofty teleported out of range while Alex raised her shield to defend her and Xenos. A group of piglins angrily swarmed around them. "Oh no! We're not wearing any gold!" exclaimed Alex. She tried to remember what Steve had told her when he had encountered a pack of them when he went to the Nether. Thinking quickly, Xenos pulled his golden necklace off his neck and threw it. All the piglin were distracted and chased after the valuable. Alex breathed a sigh of relief. The little Evoker seemed to have a few tricks up his sleeve. Lofty reunited with his friends as they walked into the temple. Everything was pitch black as soon as they walked into the entrance tunnel. Alex led the way with her torch but its light was much dimmer than usual. "Creepy." she muttered.

They continued. Soon, Alex saw a dim light ahead as it got hotter. The passage grew into a huge room. Lava lazily sloshed around at the bottom of the temple. There were mounds of soul sand everywhere on top of the blackstone. Soul lanterns were everywhere and in the middle of the room, there was a plinth. It was only connected to the rest of the temple by a bridge on either side of it. There was nothing but lava under it.

Chapter 17

A cloaked figure continued into the darkness. He wore a dull green cloak which covered his face. The stranger wore leather sandals and was hurriedly walking through a gloomy forest. There was a cave up ahead, its mouth wanting to swallow the traveller whole. But it was his only way to get to safety. The sound of mobs rustling through the bushes was clear in the cold night air. The person was holding a bundle. It looked heavy and was shaped like an egg. "You will be safe, young one." the stranger said in a voice Steve was somewhat familiar with. He sounded old and frail.

An arrow pinged behind the man. A skeleton emerged from the trees. The man started jogging slowly. He must have been quite old because he could barely keep up the pace before needing to slow down. Suddenly, a creeper jumped in front of him. It flashed white before exploding... and that was when Steve awoke.

He nearly fell out of the tree he was sleeping on. Last night, Steve had walked and walked for what seemed like an eternity. Finally, he had practically sleepwalked his way up a hill out of reach of mobs. He had climbed up to a bough of a tree and fell into slumber. He groggily climbed down and

"Okay, we can go now!" Xenos said. Alex shook her head and slowly crept forward. "I think there's something here." Alex slowly crept onto the bridge. It creaked under her weight. "Careful!" Xenos shouted. Alex leapt off the bridge and hung onto the plinth. At the top, she could feel something. Alex swung herself up and took the item. It was a small crystal, light blue in colour. What was it? Alex reckoned it was something important if it was so hard to get. Alex took the small object and was about to cross the bridge when something teleported in front of her. It was Null.

He hovered in the air for a few seconds before landing on the other side of the bridge. Null stomped his foot down on the ground and the rickety bridge collapsed into the lava, the planks melting one by one. Alex gasped. How did he find them?

"I've been waiting for a long time. But where's Steve? I thought he would come so I could finish him off! "he called. "No matter. Give me the crystal." Null pulled out his sword. Alex drew her trident. She threw it at Null who teleported to the behind her. The trident was inches away from hitting Xenos before Lofty held his hand in front of him. The trident stopped in mid-air. This was telekinesis, a power only strong and knowledgeable Enderman could wield. . Lofty sent it flying back at Null who knocked it out of the air. It jammed itself in the wall. Now Alex was weapon less. Null threw his sword at her. Alex kicked it back at him. Null ducked and the blade crashed into a pile of soul sand. A bluish-white figure emerged from the sand. It was a ghost.

This was not unusual in the Nether. The souls of the people in the Overworld ended up in the soul sand valleys of the Nether while their bodies remained in the Overworld. And the sword had just disturbed a sleeping phantom. It shrieked and flew above their heads before flying through the wall out into the Nether. Xenos screamed. As he did so, a couple of little vexes appeared. They flew over to Null and started hitting him with their swords. Being small, they didn't do much apart from annoy him. "What are these things?" he shouted. It was the perfect distraction. "Let's go!" said Alex. Along with the crystal, she grabbed Lofty's slender arm. "Get us out of here!"

Lofty attached himself to Xenos as he teleported. Null tried to reach them but Alex's trident freed itself from the wall (it was enchanted with loyalty) and flew at Null. It struck him on the leg and he fell to the floor. That was all Alex could see before they teleported out of the temple.

******

Chapter 15

Steve slowly woke up. He didn't know what happened. He had been trapped by bars, and then... he was here. He stood up and stretched his arms. Steve winced as pain stabbed through his right arm. He looked down at a nasty gash which had ripped through his shirt. Steve carefully stood up and took in his surroundings. He was in a cage. The bars were rusty and the cage was rocking from side to side. Steve looked out of the cage and gasped. The cage was in a large underground room. It was suspended from the ceiling hanging on a chain. Underneath it, there was lava.

It wasn't just any lava. It was rising lava. Every second, it grew a little closer to the cage. Steve only had minutes to escape. He was about to break out when he spotted another cage on the other side of the room. He could just make out the bedraggled, still form of his companions. Dave and Rocksteady were crammed into an identical cage. "Hey!" Steve called. Dave groaned and rolled over. He wasn't looking his best, either. A close encounter with the Warden might do that to you. At least he was alive. Rocksteady remained still.

Steve shouted again. This time, Dave lifted himself up and weakly whispered, "Hello?" Steve waved at him with his good arm. "Steve! Thank goodness you are okay!" Dave looked down and nearly screamed. "It's okay!" Steve said. "I'll get us out of this."

He had spotted a lever at the far end of the room, near his friend's cage. It could stop the lava. Unfortunately, it was just out of reach. Steve could have got to it if he could escape the cage. He searched himself for any useful tools. He didn't have much apart from a pickaxe. However, it wasn't strong enough to break the bars and was cracked in many places. It would break if he mined the bars. Still, there was one more use.

Steve took hold of the pickaxe but cried out in pain. It was too heavy for his injured arm to carry. He switched hands and hooked it around one of the bars. With all his strength, Steve wrenched away a bar. It came out with a bent end. It was just what he needed. All this while, the lava was growing ever closer...

"Dave!" Steve said. "Catch!" Steve the bar javelin-style. It was quite heavy and his left arm weaker than his right, so his throw was poor. Still, the bent end of the bar caught itself around Dave and Rocksteady's cage. Dave quickly hoisted it up before it could fall into the lava. "Now pull down the lever with it!" Steve instructed. Dave hooked the bar around the lever and pulled. The lava immediately stopped, inches away from their cages. Steve and Dave both breathed a sigh of relief. Steve saw a hole in the ceiling. He just had to get there after freeing the others.

Steve did the same for another bar which just gave him enough room to squeeze out of the cage. He placed down block after block until he was at the corner of the room. He was about to help out Dave when he said, "Steve. Stop." Steve frowned in confusion. "Don't worry about us." he continued. "We'll only get in the way; especially me. The world needs you. So get yourself out and save the world." "Ok." Steve whispered. "Don't worry; I'll stop Herobrine and find everyone. I promise." And with that, he hoisted himself out of the hole and into the darkness.

***

The sculk shrieker howled. Steve froze. He had just exited the underground room and was searching around for the book. Herobrine couldn't have just left it around but there was no harm in checking. Steve looked under the trap door again but it wasn't there. He was pretty sure Herobrine and his gang had also left as there was no sign of them. He had probably taken the book with him as well. Steve finally decided the book wasn't here so all he needed to do was escape.

But he was in an ancient city; it wasn't going to be easy. Though the portal wasn't far, one wrong mistake and it would be game over for him. Steve could just see the Nether Portal on the other side of the city. On his way there, he saw the ruins from his last battle with the Warden. It could be lurking around that corner, watching his every move...

Suddenly, he heard a crunching sound from behind him as the sculk shrieker howled for the last time. It was the sound something big and scary makes when its digging itself out of the ground. Steve groaned. He could run, or stay put. The life and death decision. He only had seconds to choose but his body made the choice for him. Steve was rooted to the spot in terror as the Warden sniffed around in the air. He couldn't help but smirk as the Warden started madly waving about in the opposite direction.

He confidently stepped back but his foot caught on a sculk censor. He fell hard on the ground.

The Warden turned around and rapidly started running at him. Steve just rolled out of the way as it slammed down on the ground, causing stone to be thrown everywhere. But it was a quick mover and blasted its sound rays at him. Steve covered his ears with his hands. He flew back into a filthy pool of water. He aimed his bow at the beast, while jumping around it in a circle. It didn't know which way to go. Then Steve would run in and ferociously swipe with his sword. The Warden retaliated with fierce blows from his fists which Steve ducked under.

But it had too much health and was too powerful. Steve was thrown back against a chest and jumped out of the way as the Warden easily split the chest in half. Something shiny and golden lay on the floor. It looked like a golden apple but more... magical. Steve clambered onto the low wall and leaped over the Warden and grabbed the apple. It was an

Enchanted Golden Apple. Steve was very low on health and instinctively ate it. He felt energy flow through him and his health was instantly restored. In fact, he had much more health than before. Steve also had resistance, which was great.

With renewed hopes, Steve fought on. The Warden quickly got rid of his extra health but not before Steve could land a few good hits on him. A diamond sword seemed powerful, but against the Warden, it was not very effective. Still, bit by bit it was losing health. The Warden abruptly released his explosive sonic boom. Steve ran for cover. It had missed him, but the sound rays broke the portal, shattering purple shards everywhere. There was only a lifeless obsidian rectangle left. "No!" Steve shouted.

There was no way out now. Steve couldn't hold off much longer against this monster. He had to do something drastic. Then an idea sparked in his head. He gathered up all the TNT in his pack and placed it all down in front of the between him and the Warden. He didn't have a flint and steel. So he hurriedly scooped lava out of a lava pool and placed it down on the TNT. Steve knew it worked when he heard the distinctive hiss of an explosive. He built up with his wooden planks so he didn't take any explosion damage. He heard a roar down below before the explosions started. All the smoke blocked his view of what was happening beneath him.

Then all was quiet. Had he beaten it at last? Out of the blue, the sound rays came at Steve through the smoke. He was falling of his tower to his doom. Thinking quick, he placed down a block beneath him to stop his fall. He heard the Warden still prowling around. How had it survived? Steve drew his bow and shot an arrow at the Warden before it sniffed him out. Surprisingly, it fell to the floor. It was gone. Steve jumped down and peered at the item lying on the ground. A sculk catalyst? After all of that? He could have just mined that!

However, that wasn't important. Steve needed to focus on getting out of the cave. That part would be easy; just dig straight up. But his pickaxe was broken so he couldn't do that. So he tried to find a way out by wondering around in the dark. Soon, he came across a mineshaft. Perfect. He got all the wood he needed from here and crafted a stone pickaxe, which he upgraded to iron after making a furnace. He could hear mobs everywhere so he gathered up as much cobblestone as he could and started building up to the cave roof.

It took many hours of mining and his new pickaxe was nearly broken, but Steve at last saw the light of the day. "Ahh!" Steve breathed in the fresh air. He looked around. Apparently he was in the middle of nowhere. He was next to a pretty sunflower field standing on a barren patch of rock facing the ocean. Steve randomly chose a direction and started walking. He was miles away from Herobrine's base, and that was where he needed to go.

Steve continued walking. He knew what he needed to find: a village. He could trade there and get a Woodland Explorer Map, which could lead him to the mansion. So Steve kept his eye out for a village. It was nearing evening when he finally spotted one. The roof of one of the houses jutted out from behind a hill. Here he could find a cartographer. A small sign said: WELCOME TO ARROWPOINT

Steve entered the village. It was similar to Daint in size. There were many villagers flocking under a large birch tree. They all looked worried and spoke in hushed whispers. "He's coming!" they whispered. Steve frowned. Who was coming? Could it be Herobrine? Suddenly, a farmer rushed up to him and grabbed his shoulders tightly. "Get out!" he cried. "Get out!"

"Just calm down-" Steve began but the farmer had already left. As Steve walked around, he noticed that all the villagers were like this. He just ignored them and tried to find a single sane person. He came across a large house. Steve entered the house. It was covered in dusty cobwebs and had maps everywhere. The chests were crammed with maps. The carpet was hidden by piles of maps. Many more were piled up on the window sill. Steve had never seen a house so chaotic. Upstairs, there was an old man. He wore a golden monocle and wore a brown tunic. He was carrying so many maps that his face was hidden under the load. "May I help you?" he asked Steve politely when he saw him.

"Uh, yeah." he replied. "I need a Woodland Explorer Map, if you have one. It's for stopping Herobrine."

The cartographer put down all the maps on a table which already had a lot of maps. He rummaged a chest and handed Steve a parchment. Steve was about to give him his compass in return but the cartographer said, "On the house. As it's for stopping Herobrine."

"Thank you!" Steve said gratefully. "Also, what's all the fuss outside about?"

The cartographer sighed. "Apparently, Arrowpoint is next on the list for Herobrine. I mean, why would he want to attack us? We've got nothing. We are just a small countryside village." Steve patted him on the back. "Don't worry. I'm sure you'll be safe." Suddenly, there was an explosion and a scream outside. Steve instantly ran outside, sword in hand. What he saw was terrifying.

Herobrine was floating over the village. The Command block was in his hand, while Entity 303 and Deathlord were attacking the village at ground level. Herobrine had the Chaos Slayer and was launching explosive energy bolts at the villagers. Arrowpoint's iron golem must have enrolled in special Herobrine training because he was fearlessly protecting the villagers and taking the hits from the Chaos Slayer. Entity 303 was right behind him with his scythe but the iron golem whirled around and slammed him into Deathlord. Next, he tore out a chunk of stone from an exposed cave and threw it at Herobrine.

He easily sliced the boulder in half but looked a little surprised. But then he placed down the Command block and summoned in masses of mobs. They were hundreds, if not thousands of zombies, skeletons and creepers. The few remaining villagers quickly disappeared in the sea of mobs. I can't let this happen, thought Steve. He equipped his armour and sliced his way into the battlefield. A zombie fell over there, a creeper drew its last hiss, and every mob was overwhelmed by Steve's strength. All of a sudden, his armour started glowing blood-red. Just like when Herobrine had hurt Shadow in the Nether. Steve eyes shone with fire. His sword felt like the ultimate weapon. Skeleton arrows pinged harmlessly off him. Steve swung his sword around in an arc and dozens of mobs fell at his feet. He felt invincible. Suddenly, he began levitating in the air, up to Herobrine's height. How was this happening? Steve was baffled but didn't have time to think. Herobrine blasted purple lightning bolts at him but Steve deflected them off the edge of his sword, frying the zombies who were unlucky enough to be in the range of the rebound blast. He threw his sword at Herobrine like a throwing axe. The hilt smacked him on the face and he flew a few meters backwards. The sword returned to Steve's hands. He flew at Herobrine and grabbed him, throwing him to the floor. He quickly got back up and flew into Steve, taking him high into the sky. There they fought. The two blades clinked together and sparks erupted around them. Steve twisted the Chaos slayer in Herobrine's hand and pushed his blade against it. Both the swords fell to the ground hundreds of meters below. Steve didn't waste time. He and Herobrine collided mid-air and they both started falling to the floor. The wind rushed past Steve. He couldn't save himself now. At least Herobrine would be going down with him.

Then a pool of water came into view. Steve kicked Herobrine away and dived towards the pond. Even in water, the landing was painful. Water exploded everywhere. Steve was vaguely aware of Herobrine who had crash-landed on the hard ground, leaving a crater full of dirt, grass and Herobrine.

Despite being in pain, Steve hobbled to the crater. Herobrine had gone. "Ah! I missed him again!" Steve growled. He saw the village still being attacked by the mobs and Herobrine's cronies. Luckily, his now dirt-encrusted diamond sword was only a few meters away, stuck in the ground. Steve pulled it out and ran to the village.

******

Chapter 16

"What is it?" Alex asked. "It's definitely not any kind of ore." She held up the item she had got at the temple. Lofty peered closely at it. 'I don't know.' he whispered. The crystal was not any normal crystal. Anyone could tell that. It glowed mystically like an enchanted sword or helmet. It was translucent white and sometimes Alex could see something moving inside it.

She held the crystal in her palm. It slowly moved around like a compass. It was pointing in one direction; maybe North. Alex checked her compass but North was in another direction. The crystal pointed roughly South East. Then it started trying to tug itself out of her hand. It was trying to go South- East, to find whatever was there. Alex tightened her grip around it and stuffed it in her pocket. "It's alive!" Xenos came forward and asked for the crystal. Alex gave it to him. "I think I've seen something like this before." he said. "In the mansion's library... something about four crystals. It gives the owner of the crystals the power to destroy anything with the touch of the Ender Axe. Apparently, they lead to each other. It must be pointing to the nearest crystal!" "That sounds pretty far-fetched. But it looks like Herobrine really wants the crystals so we should get them before him." Alex replied.

'But why would he need them? He already has the Command block. He can get whatever he needs from that.' Alex wondered. What else could Herobrine need? "Maybe it's the key to destroying the Command block! I mean, Null was obviously trying to stop us getting it." she said, remembering how close he was to getting them.

Speaking of which, her trident hadn't returned to her yet. Lofty must have teleported far away. They were back in the Overworld now. 'We only have one lead and that's to find the other crystals. So Herobrine wants it, we don't let him get it.' Alex thought. It was there only option. Null was obviously waiting for Steve to come so he could take him out if everything else that had happened wasn't enough. He had failed to get the crystal from them. Alex even felt a little sorry for Null, after Herobrine had dealt with him.

"So, we shouldn't just stand here and do nothing. Let's get the crystals!" Xenos declared and started walking North-East. Alex checked her map. It an oak forest took up most of the corner and stretched out of the map. There was nothing special about it but it looked far away. Luckily, Lofty could help a little with that. He linked arms with his companions and teleported straight into the middle of the forest. To conserve Lofty's energy, the three decided to walk the last thousand blocks which wasn't far at all from the crystal.

The three walked for an hour, when the sun was beginning to set, and Lofty began talking. 'You know, we really shouldn't worry so much about anyone else. I'm sure they're fine.'

He nudged Xenos. 'John was really tough. He must have got out of the mansion in time.' Xenos nodded sadly. "And Steve. If anyone could survive that burning mansion, he could." Alex said. "But the Village Elder and my father..." she trailed off.

Lofty sighed. Even he couldn't help feel a little down. It had been days since they had seen anyone else. With nothing else to say or do, they continued walking until they came to the edge of the forest and came across a little ruined village. Something was familiar about. Suddenly, with a jolt, Alex realised what she was looking at. It was Daint.

***

Slash! Another skeleton fell to the floor. Steve was slicing through dozens of mobs at a time. Still, they were only a distraction. Entity 303 and Deathlord walked side by side behind the crowd of monsters. Deathlord clicked his fingers and the mobs stopped spawning. He waited for Steve to finish the remaining zombies before drawing out his sword. Entity 303 readied his scythe.

Steve walked forwards. His foot scraped across something hard on the floor. It was a pile of iron ingots; all that was left of the iron golem. Steve tried not to think about it. The powerful aura around him had almost worn off. He was tired and every bit of him ached. After all, he had fallen from so high! Still, he ran at his enemies and attacked. That was the thing about Steve. He had aimlessly charged into battle without evaluating his adversary. With only one sword, Steve struggled to block the blows from them.

He barely avoided the attacks and was covered in scratches from Entity's scythe. He swung the scythe at Steve who raised his sword and blocked the attack. He kicked Entity 303 away just in time to parry Deathlord's attack. Suddenly, Entity 303 launched laser beams from his eyes at Steve. Steve blocked with his shield but the lasers had penetrated the wood and left two smoking holes.

Deathlord stabbed his sword into the ground and a fissure opened with mobs crawling out of it. Steve did his best to drive them back into the hole. Suddenly, a ghast flew out of the hole and launched a fireball at Steve. He drew his Pillager crossbow and loaded it with the single arrow he had had time to make. He jumped out of the way and the fireball hit his enemies. Through the smoke, Steve saw the dark shape of the ghast and fired. It floated down to the ground.

Steve thought that the fireball would have been enough but after the smoke cleared, Entity 303 and Deathlord were standing there, unscathed. Entity thrust his scythe in the fire and swung his flaming weapon at Steve. He jammed his sword under Entity's scythe blade and held off as long as he could.

Deathlord lunged and Steve fell back. Entity's scythe hit the ground sending a crack in the ground. Steve fell into the ravine and was only a few metres from lava before he placed down a ladder. He held onto the bottom rung with one hand. He breathed a sigh of relief. Close one! Entity 303 peered over the edge and blasted lasers at Steve. He hugged the wall as they missed and splashed in the lava. Little flecks landed on Steve but his armour protected him.

Suddenly, Steve remembered a little trick he had used in the Nether once. He dipped his sword in the lava, essentially giving it fire aspect. But the lava would cool of soon so Steve would have to act quickly. Pulling out a water bucket, Steve used Alex's handy trick and placed down some water. Steve continuously did this and reached the top of the ravine Entity had created. He jumped out and lashed at Entity 303. He landed a direct strike on his weapon arm. The sword blade was moulded blunt by the lava but it was like hitting someone with a hot rod.

Entity 303 screamed and stumbled back. Steve tripped him up and he fell into the ravine. Entity, however, had annoyingly powerful teleportation powers and disappeared with a bang. But Deathlord hadn't gone yet. He and Steve had a sword to sword duel. Steve, with his exemplary sword skills, locked his hilt under Deathlord's. He twisted with his arm and both swords fell away with a clatter. Steve punched Deathlord away from him. He made a lunge for his sword but Deathlord had other ideas. Similar to the Warden, he dug himself underground out of harm way. Steve hurriedly mined at the spot where he had disappeared but found nothing. Basically, it was Deathlord's method of teleportation.

All the battling had kept Steve busy. Then he realised how tired he was. Steve gratefully sank to the floor. He could have slept for the rest of the week but he remembered his quest and the village. Arrowpoint was now worse than the time the Wither had attacked Daint. The houses were all destroyed apart from one or two reasonably intact buildings near the edge of the village. Steve then remembered the Cartographer. He ran into his house but found nothing. Nothing except the map he had been given. Steve then realised he couldn't waste anymore time moping.

As much as it hurt him, Steve needed to leave the village before Herobrine returned to his base and he could reach his base before him. He took one final look at Arrowpoint. He couldn't save it. Then he walked away in sorrow.

******

stretched. Steve remembered last night's dream. Who was that person? What did he have to do with Steve?

Steve peered back the way he came. From his vantage point, he could barely see the remains of Arrowpoint but tried not to think about it. On the other side, he could see what was left of the mansion in the distance. He tried not to think about that, either. At least it meant he was close. Steve had a breakfast of freshly picked apples and bread from Arrowpoint's bakery chest (it was clear no one was left to sell it but Steve did leave a few gold nuggets as a sign of respect for the baker).

After he had finished, Steve was faced by the daunting problem of getting back down. Using a water bucket was a little too risky for Steve and he only used it when he had to. Ladders likewise. A hay bale was possible since he had stocked up from the village. Only a few were left that hadn't been destroyed in a shower of straw. Still, he would take some damage. Of course, he could walk all the way back down but that would take up precious time that he unfortunately didn't have. Then Steve remembered something.

He had the pair of elytra that Alex had got from the End City. It was one of the things he had hurriedly grabbed from the mansion and forgot about. But now he needed it. He swapped it out for his chestplate (which was a relief because it was quite heavy) and took out an object. His one singular firework. Lofty had shown him how he could be boosted by it when flying with elytra. He had this leftover from the flying practices he had in his free time. If he used it at the right moment then he could have just enough momentum to reach Herobrine's base in one shot.

Still, the Elytra had gotten tattered in his small rucksack. Would it work? There was only one way to find out.

Gulping, Steve jumped. He was still falling towards the dark oak forest below him before his wings caught the wind and he flew upwards a little. His stomach was doing loop the loops. Then he dived down confidently. He was about to hit giant red mushroom before he used his firework and rocketed upwards with immense speed. He was so close to the base now. Steve gently angled himself downward. He glided past Herobrine's base and landed softly on the ground.

Nobody seemed to be there. It was all clear. Steve climbed over the obsidian walls and landed in the courtyard. He had to be careful since Herobrine had advanced base safety measures. He needed to get inside the main building which was guarded by snow golems. They were trapped inside a bedrock box with enough space to shoot at any intruders. They also had fire around the opening, which meant they were basically fireball cannons. Steve slowly sneaked past them.

The solid iron door had a button which allowed Steve to easily slip inside. It was even more impressive than the outside. The whole floor was made of gold and the walls were made of something Steve had never seen before. They were polished dark black blocks which were really strong and heavy. They were Netherite blocks. Steve shook his head in disgust. It was such a waste. All of this lovely loot could have been used to help people instead of making an unnecessarily extravagant base. Why, thought Steve, couldn't he take some of it to help others?

Then Steve remembered he had come to find the book. At the end of the hall, there was a small area that had been covered up by Netherite blocks. There was a button in one of them. Steve decided to go there; this could be the location of the book. Or it could be a trap...

However, Steve didn't worry. There weren't any traps so far. Why would there be one now? Steve strolled towards the button. He pressed it without hesitation. Suddenly, an alarm started sounding. The noise pierced through Steve's ears like a knife. Unfortunately, the Netherite blocks didn't budge. Then Steve heard the hiss of lava. He looked up. A sizzling column of lava was slowly making its way down from the ceiling. Within minutes, the whole room would be overcome by it.

Thinking fast, Steve drew out his diamond pickaxe and hacked away at the Netherite. It soon came out into his hand. There was a chest in the small niche. Steve opened it and pulled out the dusty leather book. This was it. Steve ran for his life out of the huge iron doors. As he ran, Steve noticed something out of the corner of his eye. Herobrine had just teleported to the base. He had known he was here. Steve had only seen him the day before and here he was again. Would he ever leave him alone?

Not spotting Steve, he flew into his base. A few seconds later, Steve heard him bellow in anger as he realised the book was gone. Steve continued running until he was out of breath and dived into the mouth of a cave.

It was becoming night now. Totally exhausted, Steve stumbled down further into the cave. It was a dead end after walking for a couple of minutes. Steve sat down at the very end of the cave, out of sight and tried to sleep.

That night, Steve had another dream. The same man was being chased by another pack of mobs. A skeleton with an enchanted bow drew his weapon and fired an arrow at the stranger. It hit him in the fleshy part of his leg, which was lucky but he still fell to the floor and dropped the bundle in front of him. A small black object rolled out. It was the dragon egg from Daint. Why did that man have it? Suddenly, the egg began to shake and started to crack. Then the egg broke apart completely. There was a brilliant shower of purple light... before the dream ended.

******

Chapter 18

Alex carefully picked her way through the sea of rubble- all that was left of Daint. She was on the verge of tears. Her beautiful village, all gone. Nothing could have caused this but Herobrine. She noticed a pile of birch planks- Steve's house. All of the keepsakes from her and Steve's adventures were scattered around the ruined house. But something was missing- the dragon egg. But at this point Alex couldn't care less.

Lofty and Xenos came to stand by Alex. "Hey, do you hear that?" asked Xenos. Something was moving around in a pile of cobblestone. Alex picked up one of Steve's swords from the ground. Xenos shivered in fear. Alex gradually and vigilantly edged towards the pile of stone. Abruptly, a small figure leaped out from the rubble. It hissed at them. Alex was about to attack, before recognizing the creature. It was Shadow. Alex almost couldn't identify her at first. Shadow was very thin and limped slightly. She was covered from head to toe in dust, giving her coat a dirty grey colour.

Alex dropped the sword and picked Shadow up. Xenos ran to a fallen barrel and shook it open. It was filled with fresh fish. He tossed Shadow one. She devoured it like a hungry wolf. Xenos tipped the rest of the barrel over. Shadow continued her much-needed feast while the three searched the buildings. Alex found a zombie leatherworker wandering around. She couldn't stand it. Enough was enough. Alex ran towards the nearest brewery and rummaged through the chests. There was a fermented spider, some gunpowder and a glass bottle. She filled up the bottle from the lake and dragged a brewing stand out of the debris. It was very battered and the arms were damaged but Alex would have to make do. Luckily, the stand had enough charge left in it. Alex mixed together the water bottle and the fermented spider eye. She now had a potion of weakness. Adding the gunpowder, she waited while the potion brewed. Now she had a splash potion weakness. Alex found the zombie villager shuffling around the edge of the lake. She tossed him the golden apple before it could attack. Puzzled, the zombie villager ate the apple. Alex threw the splash potion of weakness at it.

The zombie began to shake. Within minutes, there was a normal lady standing where the zombie had been. The cure had worked! "Thank you!" she said to Alex.

Alex smiled. "It was nothing. What happened?" The lady began telling her story. "A few weeks after you and Steve left, Null and Herobrine came. They destroyed the village, asking about Steve. Nobody gave you guys up so Herobrine attacked us."

Alex didn't want to tell the woman that there was no point in hiding their location. Herobrine had found them anyways. Instead, she said, "What about the iron golem? He could have protected you." The lady shook her head. "He tried his best. But what is one iron golem compared to Herobrine? Thank goodness, he is still here. Let me show you."

The lady took Alex into the forest. The iron golem was slumped against a tree trunk. He was covered in vines, which showed things weren't going good for him. "It's okay. Let me help you!" Alex said. She gave the iron golem some iron ingots which healed him up. Alex continued. "I won't be here to help so it's your responsibility to help protect and find any villagers." The iron golem nodded seriously.

"What about you?" the lady asked.

"I'm sorry, I can't stay long. But Herobrine won't come back again. So you will be safe." The lady nodded. Lofty nudged Alex. 'The crystal.' Alex nodded and went back to the village. She pulled out her crystal. It pointed to the middle of the debris, at Steve's house. Alex, Lofty and Xenos dug under the birch planks when Alex felt something hard in the ground. It was a chest. Alex scrabbled around it until she could lift it out of the hole. In the chest was a scroll.

Alex unrolled it. Inside was the second crystal. "Yes!" she exclaimed. She grabbed the other one from her pocket and connected it with the second one like a jigsaw. The crystal glowed brighter than ever. Then she unrolled the scroll. It said:

'To whoever finds this, the next crystal lies in the depths below, where he will be waiting.'

"What? That's it?" Xenos asked. "In the depths below, where he will be waiting..." Alex rolled up the parchment and put it in her pocket. "Ok. It's goodbye sunshine, hello darkness."

***

"Again!" Rocksteady smashed his horn into the cage. They barely made a dent on the iron. Rocksteady stumbled to the floor. He was exhausted. The stump left of his other horn was taking ages to grow back. It had been days since Steve had left and they were running out of food. To Dave, it was like being trapped in the End all over again. But this time, there was no hope of getting help. They were trapped.

******

Chapter 19

Steve awoke in the morning cold and stiff. He still had the book, which was good. But he needed to get away from Herobrine's base as quickly as possible. Steve walked through the forest, further and further away. The column of smoke rising from the base finally disappeared. When he seemed far enough away, Steve opened the book and began to read. At first, there were no words and Steve thought he had been duped but elaborate thin words slowly appeared on the yellowing pages.

'It is the crystal you seek, head South from here. Once the four merge the Ender axe's wrath none can withstand. Once you find the first, you will need me no more. Prevent the world's end, our blessing we send.'

So ominous... Herobrine did mention the Ender axe though, so maybe the whole thing wasn't a sick joke. Steve needed to head south. That meant going back in the opposite direction. This time, Steve took a long curve around Herobrine's base. There wasn't much of a place to hide since most of the forest had been burned away.

Suddenly, Steve saw something out of the corner of his eye. It had seen him as well. Steve began running into the woods.

Herobrine had found him yet again. But there was no sound above him of Herobrine chasing him.

Steve sneaked a peak upwards. Small red block were falling from the sky. As they got closer, Steve saw what they were. TNT! Herobrine had summoned a TNT rain again! The whole forest was going up in smokes. Steve used his fishing rod to drag a TNT towards him and using the momentum of the blast, he flew up into the air.

He quickly equipped his elytra in mid-air and glided in between the falling TNT. Steve was invincible! But then, disaster struck. The explosive rain was fading and Steve was confident that he was going to make it out.

The wind dropped and Steve was slowing down. Then a TNT exploded next to him and he was hurtled across the skies. He had no idea how far he had travelled with his eyes tearing up in the wind but he was moving very fast. Steve crash-landed in a mangrove forest and fell through the many roots in a tangle. He fell into the shallow, murky swamp in an explosion of water. Steve didn't move. His head throbbed and he was pretty sure his ankle had been twisted.

At last, he tried to pull himself out of the tangle of roots. However, the more he pulled, the more tangled he got. Soon Steve gave up and hung limply in the same spot. Steve tried to get his sword so he could cut himself out but his sword, along with the book was sitting at the bottom of the pond. Then Steve got an idea. He could just reach into his shirt pocket and get his flint and steel. He could burn away the tree roots. It was risky, but worth a shot. It took many tries with the damp roots but Steve managed to set alight the nearest root near his arm. It curled away into smoke and burned through the other roots as well. Steve fell into the swamp, free.

Not wasting any time, Steve grabbed his sword and cut the elytra out of the mess of roots which he had left behind. Before started to fly again, Steve fought his way out of the forest and walked for a little while, drying off. He soon came across a little beach. It was hidden by the tall, majestic mangrove trees and illuminated by the brilliant golden sun.

A turquoise ocean stretched out for many miles. Steve sat down on the white sand. Near the water, there was a cluster of green plants. It was sugarcane. Steve realised how this could be useful and gathered all of it. He turned it into paper. Using this and some gunpowder, he could make more fireworks.

So Steve waited until night time when the creepers appeared. He started attacking them for their gunpowder. Since he had lost his shield when he went flying into the mangrove forest, it was a lot harder. Steve had to be quick and take out the creepers before they could sense him.

Most of them exploded, but by morning Steve got a good haul of gunpowder. He crafted all of them together with the paper and had a fresh stack of fireworks. He used one of the fireworks and zoomed upwards. He needed to head south like the book said. When he pulled the book out of the swamp, it was sopping wet and the writing was illegible, so he left it where it was.

By late afternoon Steve was still flying. He had stopped at a couple of places, restocking fireworks and hunting for food.

It had been ages since he was flying over the plains. Luckily, Steve could spot a jungle biome up ahead. Strangely, there was something familiar about the jungle. It was like he had been here, in this very jungle before...

Steve continued flying but didn't see anything special. After flying for another couple of minutes, the feathers from his elytra started coming apart. It was breaking! Steve tried his best to get to the ground but the elytra broke and he was still high above the ground.

Since leaves could be waterlogged, Steve couldn't use his bucket. Instead, he looked out for any vines. Steve grabbed on to one as he was falling and slid down it. He dropped to the floor, avoiding letting his left ankle take the strain. He checked his compass and continued south. Progress was ten times slower than when he was flying, especially with his leg. Spasms of pain passed through his leg with every step. After walking for a while, Steve reached a riverside. It was very familiar. Then he realised it was where he had tamed Shadow and seen Lofty for the first time. It was the very same jungle he had quested in to find the Totem of Undying. Just behind that tree...

Steve smiled at the memory and continued walking. All day he trekked through the undergrowth until the sun began to set. He climbed a tree and looked down upon the green canopy. Steve spotted a glimmer in a small clearing. He descended down the trees and walked towards it. It was a small lake. Steve looked at the beautiful surroundings and felt the atmosphere of mystery around him. It was the Legendary Lake.

At the bank, there was a rotting wooden boat stuck in the mud. Steve pulled it out and recognized it as his own. He climbed into it and started rowing to the middle of the lake. The plinth which held the totem of undying was still there but instead a small, glowing object sat on the surface. But Steve had forgotten about one minor detail...

The tip of a trident poked up into the deck. The old boat fell apart and Steve was suddenly underwater, his armour weighing him down into the bottomless lake. A Drowned with a trident was swimming towards him. They were the guardians of the lake. Another one appeared and grabbed Steve by the leg and pulled him under the water. Steve kicked him and slashed with his sword. The sea creature floated to the bottom of the lake.

Steve kicked upwards and gasped for air. He scrambled onto the little island in the middle of the lake. It would be easier than last time, since most of the Drowned had been defeated by the Enderman and Piglins. Steve reckoned there were only about two hundred left. One by one, the Drowned emerged from the water. Steve's high- class armour protected him from the tridents and using his bow, Steve could take out the Drowned hiding underwater. At last, there was only one left.

He had a trident which glowed a faint purple. It was enchanted. Suddenly, he propelled himself through the air and landed behind Steve. The trident was enchanted with riptide, unlike Alex's which had Loyalty. The mobs thrust his trident at Steve, who met it with his sword. Steve pushed the trident down and kicked the Drowned back into the water. The monster propelled himself down into the depths of the water. Steve aimed his crossbow and scored a direct hit on the Drowned. It sank to the ground. Steve dived underwater and yanked the trident out of its hands. Steve boosted himself back near the plinth. He looked down in wonder at the crystal before taking it. That wasn't too hard.

Like Alex's crystal, this crystal spun around until it pointed North West at a slight gradient. Steve immediately knew what that meant. He put the crystal in his pocket and started walking. He was so close.

******

Chapter 20

"Oh, you're coming too, are you?" Alex, Xenos and Lofty had just left the village until they realized Shadow was following them. She mewed. Shadow had been given a wash in the lake and was properly fed. She had apparently forgotten about her feline friends, who fled into the forest at the sound of Herobrine's footsteps. Since she was now in top condition, Alex allowed her to come. Like Steve's, the crystal was angling down. It was the final crystal. They were both heading to the same place!

The final crystal was either underground or in the Nether. Alex reckoned it would be somewhere underground instead of in the Nether because they had already found one there. So the four of them started walking towards their destination. Alex couldn't help feel excited. There were two more left for her to find, though she didn't know Steve had already found one. And after all that business was sorted, she could rebuild Daint, find her father, the Village Elder and Steve and they could live happily ever after... (Cough, cough). With Herobrine in the world, there would be no happy ending.

After walking for some time, Alex said, "I think I know where we're going. It's pointing to the same direction as the cave with the ancient city in." Lofty could easily teleport them there!

But before they could progress further, they heard a sound in the air. Instinctively, Alex yelled, "Duck!" They all jumped into a bush. Alex brushed her hair out of her eyes and looked up. A small, dark figure was flying hundreds of blocks above. It was Null.

He was heading in the same direction as them. 'After him!' Lofty said. Under the cover of the trees, they followed him. Null was fast, so Lofty had to keep teleporting the others to keep up with him. Soon they reached the cave, as expected. Null flew in and disappeared. The group ventured into the cave. It was very dark so Xenos sent ahead little vexes to check their position.

Once or twice they nearly walked into a lava pit, or a skeleton dungeon (Alex managed to find some golden apples for the fight guaranteed ahead). The cobblestone turned into deepslate, and soon they had fell into complete darkness. Suddenly, Xenos stumbled over the wet cave floor and Lofty caught him before teleporting out of the water. Xenos knocked into Alex as Lofty let go of him, who tripped over Shadow and they were all falling, deeper and deeper. Luckily Lofty managed to hold onto a vine. The rest clung on underneath him. But they couldn't stay like this for long. On cue, the vine began to snap... and they were suddenly all lying on wool. Wool? Thought Alex. Then she realized where they were. In the Ancient City.

Alex immediately started digging down. The crystal must be around here somewhere, she thought. Then she heard something. There was someone shouting for help. It was Dave! She could recognize his voice anywhere. Alex, without caring about the sculk sensors, ran towards the sound.

The sensors howled. Alex began digging down and fell into a cage and got a huge shock. Inside, there was a very gaunt Dave sitting in the corner. Next to him, Rocksteady lay unmoving. Lofty teleported inside the cave and grabbed on to Dave and teleported out. Alex coaxed Rocksteady awake with some mushrooms. He ate them and Lofty was able to rescue him, too.

Soon they were all reunited. Shadow was very suspiciously eying Rocksteady while Dave and Alex chatted. "What happened to Steve?" Alex asked.

"He escaped. I hope he's safe-" Suddenly, everything went dark. "Oh no!" whispered Dave. The only source of light was Lofty's bright purple eyes. 'Follow me,' he said to the others. The message was clear in their heads. Xenos was petrified. He thought he saw something move in the darkness when-

Crash! The Warden smashed apart the wooden lookout post and charged at them. Within seconds, Rocksteady and the Warden were locked together in a duel. Alex knew how powerful ravagers were but even Rocksteady couldn't last long against the Warden. The beast was ramming its horns into the Warden. The Warden, at exactly the right moment, unleashed its sonic boom full into Rocksteady's face. The momentous Ravager went flying into the remains of the lookout post, which crashed over him.

Alex screamed. Lofty dived into the wreckage and grabbed hold of Rocksteady. He held his hand out, pointing to a rock. It began to float in the air. Lofty sent it crashing into the Warden who roared with rage.

'Hurry!' he said. Everybody clung on to Lofty as he teleported. "AAAHHH!" they screamed as they were hurtled through space. They all ended up in a bedraggled heap in the middle of a warped forest. Lofty was lying on the floor, exhausted. Alex knew why. Whenever Lofty teleported through dimensions, he became incredibly tired. But why where they here?

Alex pulled the crystal out of her pocket. Surprisingly, it was pointing straight ahead. The last crystal was in the Nether ! But they couldn't go yet. Lofty was too tired. A few other Enderman teleported around them. They asked what happened, and tried to help Lofty. Out of the corner of her eye, Alex saw lava pouring into the forest. This was common in the Nether; most of it was made from seas of lava. Even so, they didn't have much time.

The other Enderman saw the lava, and teleported to a safer place. They said to Alex, 'Continue. He will join you when he is ready.' Alex, along with Rocksteady, Dave, Xenos and Shadow, started cautiously walking the last leg of their journey.

Chapter 21

Steve was making slow progress. The Netherite block was very heavy. He stopped for a break and placed it down. What did it do? Steve found that he could turn it into Netherite ingots in his crafting table. As he inspected the heavy ore, Steve remembered what they could do. The armourer back in Daint combined these with diamond armour to make Netherite armour.

Steve needed a smithing table first, so he crafted it with two iron and cobblestone. Excited, he took off all his armour and began transforming all the diamond into Netherite. The armour felt much stronger and it was heavier as well. Steve did the same for his pickaxe and sword. The sword had a new sharp edge and was no longer blunt.

As it was evening, a spider fell from the trees and began attacking Steve. He sliced and the spider fell. Next, he tried out his armour on some zombies. They couldn't make a scratch. The Netherite pickaxe was just as good, mining blocks within seconds. Now all properly suited up, Steve continued walking to the last crystal.

It was now dead in the middle of the night. The crystal was now pointing directly down. Steve took out his pickaxe and started digging. He had found nothing apart from some lapis when he reached bedrock after a considerable amount of time. The crystal was pointing down further, below the bedrock. That mean the final crystal was in the Nether or falling for eternity in the Overworld void.

Steve decided to go back to the surface, where he had spotted a ruined portal. It was some way off but it was the only way to get to the Nether and Steve didn't have any obsidian. The ruined portal had enough obsidian to complete the portal and there were only a couple of crying obsidian pieces to remove before the portal was complete.

Steve took a deep breath and entered the portal.

***

The warped forest soon merged into the Nether wastes. The crystal was almost leaping out of Alex's steady grip. The wastes were clear of any mobs. Up ahead, Alex saw some figures standing in the gloom. As they got closer, Alex made out all of Herobrine's gang. Along with that, she got a nasty shock. The Wither had returned for battle. It was in good condition and as terrifying as ever. The last time she had saw the beast was in the Nether fortress where Steve had set it on fire.

It had healed over time and looked at its strongest. Along with the Wither, there was an army of Wither skeletons. Charging into battle was fatal. Instead, Alex and Xenos, who were both armed with bows (Xenos not able to rely on his Evoker attacks), unleashed a volley of arrows upon the army.

Most of them fell but their position was given away. All heads turned to the five warriors. Herobrine settled down on the ground with something hanging on a chain around his neck. The last crystal!

Now Alex understood what, 'He is waiting for you' meant. This was going to be the battle of all battles. Alex painfully remembered Jay and his sacrifice to defeat Herobrine. Alex hoped nobody would have to do that. But before they could battle, she heard a voice behind her.

"Alex?" said Steve. Alex nearly leaped with joy. Steve was alive! He looked formidable with his Netherite sword in hand. "Steve!" Alex ran up to him. "What happened?" "I-" Steve began but their enemies didn't give them a moment. The group, now stronger than ever, willingly ran into battle. Rocksteady crashed into dozens of skeletons while the Wither barraged it with its skulls. Steve niftily avoided them and engaged in combat with Herobrine, trying to get at the crystal.

Entity 303 shot his lasers into the chaos, mainly frying the wither skeletons, luckily for Steve and the rest. But they just kept on coming. The Wither blasted skulls at Alex who was hit several times. She was withering away so quickly ate a golden apple. She got a regeneration boost and shot arrow after arrow at the Wither. Hiding behind a Netherrack cliff, Xenos shot his arrows into the wither skeletons. Dave was armed with an iron axe and was duelling with Deathlord. Suddenly, a bunch of Enderman (not including Lofty) teleported into the battle. Each of them took one Wither skeleton each, leaving their allies to focus on the bigger threats. Steve was fiercely slashing at Herobrine but he had the Chaos Slayer. The sword ripped his shield (which he had newly crafted) out of his hand, leaving Steve defenceless. Steve grabbed the trident he had got from the Drowned and duel-wielded his weapons. Herobrine grabbed Steve and slammed him into a wall. Large chunks of Nether rack fell from the top and Steve dodged out of the way of them.

Herobrine caused chains to wrap around Steve who, with immense effort, broke free. He blocked Herobrine's sword with his trident and thrust his sword forwards. Herobrine teleported behind him and used his energy balls and blasted them at Steve. The electricity attack threw him back into the main battle. Alex was stabbing away at Null with her trident while Shadow clawed at the Wither skeletons, who couldn't hit the small ocelot.

Rocksteady was the first to fall. After smashing through another couple of Wither skeletons, the Wither ambushed him with its skulls. Rocksteady, already weak, couldn't handle the Wither poison. He fell to the floor. Nobody had noticed because they were too busy fighting. He lay there in the midst of the fight.

Herobrine had the Command block and tapped on a button. Everything went dark. A Warden appeared in the gloom. Everyone paused. The confused boss looked around. He then dug himself underground to everyone's relief.

Deathlord had just sliced Dave on the arm. He fell back in pain. Steve jumped in front of him as Deathlord slashed. His blade scarred Steve's armour who, unharmed, pushed his sword into Deathlord. He looked surprised for a second, before crumbling to dust.

Steve helped Dave up and gave him a golden apple. "Thank you." Dave whispered. Steve smiled.

"You did well." The deep cut on Dave's arm healed itself. At this point, there were lots of ender pearls lying around from fallen Enderman. Steve grabbed one and teleported on top of the Wither who had just blasted Alex over the cliff. An Enderman grabbed her at the last second.

The Wither tried to shake him off but Steve stabbed his sword into one of its skulls and grabbed on. But he was thrown off and brutally hit the ground. Without any time to heal, the Wither launched a huge blue skull at Steve. He went skidding up to Herobrine, who was tinkering with the Command block.

Steve, sword less, pulled out an arrow from the ground and stabbed it into his leg. It didn't do much damage but Herobrine was momentarily distracted. Steve leapt on top of him, pummelling Herobrine with his fists. He wrenched the crystal from Herobrine just as the lava wave Herobrine had been summoning crashed upon the two of them.

Herobrine was unharmed but Steve was burning in the lava. He dug down and blocked off the lava. Steve ate a golden apple which luckily gave him fire resistance. He swam up the lava and his fire protection ended just as he got out. But Herobrine wasn't done. He used the Command block to send a gigantic magma cube at Steve. It jumped across the lava and landed on top of him. Steve used an ender pearl and teleported away. He finished the magma cube with a volley of arrows which annihilated the smaller magma cubes easily.

Steve then bottled down a lingering potion of strength and felt the energy flowing through him.

Alex saw that Steve had the last crystal and tossed her two crystals over the sea of fighters. Steve caught them and combined the four together. The four merged together in white light. There was a beautiful axe in his hands, full of energy. It was glowing purple, with a deadly sharp double-head. Steve thrust it into the ground and created a bright explosion which blew Herobrine away into the sea of lava. But it wasn't powerful enough. He needed to get to the Command block. Herobrine rose with his sword in hand. He sent a purple electricity bolt at Steve who raised the axe to defend himself. But the electricity somehow coiled itself around the axe and Steve dropped it.

The Ender Axe began to shake. Steve could only watch helplessly as the axe burst apart into tiny shards. All their hard work! From each of those shards, a transparent, silvery form arose. They were spirits of people. Most of them shrieked and flew away. Steve recognized one of them. It was John. Suddenly, another familiar figure flew up ahead. It had short brown hair, it held a crossbow- could it be? Steve's thoughts evaporated as Xenos left his hiding spot and ran up to him. "How?" he cried. "What happened?" John shook his head sadly. "Alas, I perished in the great fire, along with our mansion. As my last request, defeat Herobrine for me." Without saying another word, John flew away into the depths of the Nether. Steve watched with his mouth open.

The only way of defeating Herobrine was gone.

******

Chapter 22

Null swiftly engaged with Alex in battle. They both wounded each other but Alex was worse off. Null was armed with two swords. He threw one at Alex. She ducked and the sword flew into a Wither skeleton, who, amazingly, dropped a wither skull. Alex took the skull and swapped it for her helmet. She looked terrifying. Alex and Null sprinted at each other. At the same time, they ran their weapons into each other.

There was a moment of silence. Then Null began to curl away like wisps of smoke, until there was nothing left of him. Alex fell to her knees and pulled out his sword, tossing it aside. Xenos ran up to her. Suddenly, the Wither launched its skulls at both of them. Xenos fell to one side and Alex was thrown across the barren wasteland like a ragdoll.

The Wither turned to face the injured Evoker. What chance did he have against that monstrous boss? Then Xenos remembered everyone Herobrine had hurt. He couldn't let that happen. Xenos's eyes were glowing golden. "YOU WILL NOT HURT MY FRIENDS!" he roared. Massive spikes rose from the ground smashing into the Wither creating a whirlwind of dust around the two of them. Unseen, there was an explosion of energy as the Wither met its end.

When the dust cleared, there was an object lying on the floor. A Nether star. Steve's sword skidded towards him. A few blocks away, Xenos was crawling towards the small golden object on the ground. His Totem of Undying. Just as he was about to reach it, he fell limp. In horror, Alex ran forward and tried to shake him awake. There was no response. She couldn't believe it: Xenos had sacrificed himself just like Jay had!

Alex sombrely picked up the totem and equipped it. Suddenly, a dark shadow fell over her. A Wither skeleton was just about to cut her down with its stone sword. Then something happened. The Wither skeletons, which had been fighting the Enderman, Dave and Shadow, disintegrated as their master perished. Dave and Shadow sighed with relief. They were both hurt and attended to their wounds while the battle raged on.

Herobrine had summoned in spikes like Xenos's, only smaller and rammed them into Steve and slightly cracked his armour. Steve was dazed. He could see Herobrine with his sword, about to shoot a bolt of electricity at him-

Pop. Something had teleported nearby. It was Lofty. He was healed! He immediately saw that Steve was in trouble and teleported in front of him just as Herobrine unleashed his attack. Steve watched with shock as Lofty took the fatal blow. It was so bright... Steve looked away. And that was that. One of Steve's best friends, his saviour, his guide, gone.

There lay a single ender pearl where he was standing. Herobrine laughed at the look of dismay on Steve's face.

But something was happening. He levitated in the air, radiating more energy than ever before. His eyes were white-hot with rage. For a second, Herobrine was scared. Then they met each other head-on but it was clear where the power lay. Steve punched his nemesis so hard that Herobrine created a landslide of blocks as he slammed into the cliff.

Alex, Dave and Shadow huddled together for safety but Entity 303 was swept away into the lava lake with a scream. Herobrine quickly sent another, larger lava wave into Steve who was submerged. Alex shouted worriedly. Steve, battered, rose from the lava. His armour had melted away from him. Herobrine drew out his sword and attacked Steve as soon as he was on the ground. Unbelievably, he caught the Chaos Slayer with his bare hands and snapped it like a matchstick. The energy crackling through it died away. Herobrine screamed angrily as his prized possession was destroyed.

Herobrine punched Steve to the edge of the cliff and his sword fell into the lava.

Herobrine and Steve were both nearing the cliff edge as they battled, fist to fist, hurtling each other across the ground. Steve felt the energy running through him. He could end this. Alex, Dave and Shadow, the only ones left from the fight, didn't interfere with the intense fight. Unnoticed, Alex ran to the Command block and took it.

Steve kicked Herobrine to the very edge of the cliff, right above the lava. His weight caused the ledge to crumble. Steve roared and leaped into Herobrine, taking them both down into the lava.

It was as if time itself slowed down. Steve and Herobrine were both falling to their end. Steve saw Herobrine fall into the lava, only seconds before he met the same fate—something flew down towards him. Alex was standing on the edge of the cliff and had thrown down the totem. Just as he made contact with the lava, the totem burst into a shower of green.

Alex anxiously waited at the top of the cliff. Had it worked? Then from behind her, she heard Shadow mew happily. There was Steve, singed and bruised but very much alive. Xenos's Totem had saved him. They had done it! But that wasn't the only surprise. Something was approaching them from the distance. As it grew closer, Steve could more clearly make out its details. It was the figure from Steve's dream. "Who are you?" Steve said shakily. The stranger took down his hood. "Sorry I was late!" Steve couldn't be happier. It was the Village Elder. He had survived. They were all happily reunited and victorious. "Uh, one more question, Elder. This might be a bit random, but I was wondering..." Steve asked.

The Village Elder looked up. "Yes?"
"What's your name?"
The Village Elder stared at Steve. "It's Tom."

******

Epilogue

"What do we do with this little fellow?" Steve asked. Him, Alex, Dave, Shadow and the Village Elder were all back in Daint. Steve had just overcome the shock of seeing his village destroyed but Herobrine was to never trouble them again.

The Village Elder, or Tom, stroked the baby Ender Dragon. Apparently, he had returned to the village after Herobrine attacked the mansion and taken the egg with him when Daint had been destroyed.

He was the one who had found one of the crystals and left it in the chest buried underground and wrote the message. After that, he followed them down into the Nether. "We take it back to where he belongs. The End." Steve nodded.

"But first we have another task." He climbed up the rocky mountain that overlooked the sea. It was all so peaceful. Not so long ago, Minecraft was a warzone against Herobrine. Three of their dear friends had gone down fighting for the safety of the Overworld. Alex handed him the Command block. They had decided it was the safest option for everyone. Steve took a deep breath and hurled it as far away as he could. It was gone forever. All their worries left them as the Command block was lost forever in the endless oceans.

Or was it?

THE END

About the Author

Abir is a young author and lives in England. His love for writing started from a young age and he is an avid reader and never took it as a task but classes it as something that relaxes him!

He was the head boy of his primary school and recently started grammar school. He has recently graded to black belt in Martial Art. His books can be enjoyed by young readers and adults.

He inherited his writing genes from his maternal grandmother who is a writer herself.

He is a scout and has been associated with it for more than 7 years. He is a fun loving young boy, liked and loved by his teachers and friends. Abir is a Lego fan, enjoys video games. He is a foodie at heart and is never behind from trying new dishes. Abir is deeply attached to his parents and younger brother who always encourages and supports him to follow his dreams.

Website: www.abirgupta.co.uk